THESE SAVAGE FUTURIANS

BOOKS BY PHILIP E. HIGH

THESE SAVAGE FUTURIANS

Philip E. High

To

Denis

With the compliments of the author

Philip E. High

COSMOS BOOKS
An Imprint of Wildside Press
New Jersey • New York • California • Ohio

THESE SAVAGE FUTURIANS

First Cosmos Books edition: December, 2000

ISBN: 1-58715-238-X

H‍E STOOD on a high white cliff looking out across the sea. Far out, clumps of weed and wreckage drifted slowly down the channel looking, in the blue-gray water like the backs of sleeping dolphins.

Closer to shore an old plastic paddle-boat butted stubbornly against the current, making such slow progress it appeared almost stationary.

He had once seen the inside of a paddle-boat. He could imagine the drive-men crouched over the bars, faces dewed with sweat and pedaling desperately to stop the vessel losing way.

"What are you doing here?"

He stiffened then turned slowly. "Please?"

"You heard me—what are you doing here?"

"I was looking at the sea."

"And why are you not at work?"

"It is my free day." He fumbled in his pocket for the pass and handed it over.

He was a tall young man with a thin tanned face, dark untidy hair and intelligent blue eyes. His body appeared thin but was strong and lithely muscled.

The questioner studied him briefly and examined the pass.

5

A certain slowness of movement and the slightly halting speech had already been noted.

The pass was in order and was handed back.

"Identity disc." The questioner waited while the other fumbled the disc from his clothing and finally extended it from the chain which encircled his neck.

The identity disc bore no writing or symbols. It was a circle of metal into which had been punched a large number of holes. The questioner ran blunt brown fingers across its surface. The holes, varying in size and arrangement, gave a complete picture of the disc's owner—*ROBERT VENTNOR. AGE 27. AGRICULTURAL LABORER. UNMARRIED. PSYCHIATRIC CLASSIFICATION 225/9/446.* At the side of the disc three separate perforations gave a psycho-genetic warning—P/D/G.

Ventnor's father had been destroyed for gadgeteering and it was apparent that this tendency had been carried forward to the next generation. Worse, although latent, the characteristic was predominant and increasing. The questioner had already decided that something must be done about it.

"Where are you going?"

"To Gret."

"That is not your village."

"True, but there is a girl—"

"It is unwise to pursue the women of other villages."

"There is no law against it, Padre."

"And no law to protect you if the males of that village take offence at your intrusion." The Padre turned abruptly and walked away. A squat man, wearing the traditional black of his kind, with a curious circle of unbroken white about his throat, he wore also a round hat with an upcurled brim which never seemed to leave his head.

Ventnor watched him go with a feeling of relief. He had heard that Padres, long ago, had been men of honor, healers and dispensers of mystery. Today, however, they were watchdogs, spies and the administrators of summary justice.

He turned slowly in case the Padre was still watching and began to trudge in the direction of Gret. He was, in truth, neither slow nor halting of speech but he had carefully cultivated these mannerisms since the age of eighteen.

6

His father had been voluble, swift of movement, eager and inquisitive. Characteristics which, in the long run, had killed him or, at least, helped.

Ventnor senior had been clever with his hands and instead of confining himself to simple carpentry had improvised and created. Nothing startling, an original door-catch, a planting implement, a swing-hinge—enough to set him apart as a gadgeteer, enough for them to mark him.

Once marked there had been nothing to do but wait; there was no point in running. No one saw the marker come and no one saw it go but there had been a flash—

Ventnor shuddered slightly, he still remembered it vividly. His father drinking from a plastic cup and suddenly—suddenly nothing. A flash, the cup spinning in a little circle on the hard floor and a few flakes of white ash drifting down from nowhere.

Of deliberation Ventnor junior had made himself slow of movement and halting of speech. He rejected his apprenticeship and volunteered for cultivation. At the time it had seemed far safer.

He had often regretted it, but he had carefully kept to himself the inner urges of creation—the desire to improvise, improve or construct from his own original fund of ideas.

They knew, of course, Robert Ventnor was a gadgeteer; that was why they had marked his disc P/D—Potential Danger.

Ventnor looked out across the sea again. Somewhere out there was the Island—the Island of the Masters.

He was wrong; the Island was in the Atlantic, but no one had told him that. As far as he knew it was beyond the horizon and often on a clear day he had felt a frightened awe when the coast of France became visible.

He came to a line of whitened stones marking the boundaries of his village and quickened his pace. It was a long walk to Gret with continuous hills and then a long winding path down to the sea.

When he reached it the scene was familiar, men tilling the small cultivation patches, garments fluttering in a brisk wind from the sea. Women were filling plastic baskets with bright green newly cut *protages* and swaying away with them balanced on their heads.

7

As he approached the men paused in their work and stared. They stared with an open-mouthed and uncomprehending intensity as if he had three arms or two heads and he felt a twinge of alarm. Previously they had only glanced and turned away, now their eyes were fixed on him unblinkingly.

He felt himself coloring and knew that his step was faltering slightly. This was a warning—a traditional warning—and, clearly they had been expecting him.

Mentally he hesitated. Now was the time to go back, now, if he returned, the men would stop staring and continue with their work. If he did not turn back, however, a warning would be shouted down to the village below and, when he arrived, men of his own age would be there to greet him—violently.

His common sense told him to go back and a stubborn pride told him to go on. After all Elseth had promised, on his last rest, on his last visit, she had promised.

He had looked down at her, gripping her shoulder. "You will be my woman? You will come and house with me?"

"Your woman, Robert Ventnor? Yes—yes, I will be your woman—if you are strong enough to take me."

He had known what she meant. Any other male who might desire her would try and stop him. At the time, inflamed by her promise, he had dismissed the problem as trivial, now—now he was not so sure.

He was tall, strong, reasonably swift of movement, but it might not be just one suitor, it might be several.

On the other hand, if he turned back, the word would quickly be passed on. They would call him 'white-stomach' and the women, the children, and the young girls would mock him openly when he returned.

Robert Ventnor stuck out his chin, lengthened his step and followed the long winding path to the village of Gret.

He thought, dully, that it would not be a good place to escape from. It would be up-hill and often between gullies in the chalk. If he lost it would be a hard, bitter and wearing retreat—if he made it.

When he reached the village she was leaning against one of the huts, smiling. She wore a shiny black plastic skirt and a sleeveless orange blouse. Copper bangles adorned

8

her wrists and ankles and her toes curled in the dust of the street.

When she saw him she tossed her head challengingly and put her hands on her hips. There was no affection in her eyes but they were bright with anticipation.

"You have come, Robert, boy."

"I have come to take you as my woman."

"If you are strong enough." She laughed shrilly. "Many suitors desire me here."

It was then that Corby came round the corner of the hut. Ventnor had met Corby once at an inter-village festival and had never liked him.

Corby had little black eyes and a ginger moustache, the ends of which he had waxed so that they stood up at right angles to the corners of his mouth. It made him look like a wild boar. Corby had squat shoulders and short but bulgy freckled arms.

He smiled, looking more like a boar than ever. "What you want here, Del, boy—what you want here?"

When he saw that no answer was forthcoming, he charged. Ventnor hit him full in the mouth as he came in and Corby staggered, little eyes glazing. Ventnor hit him again and this time Corby dropped to his knees and began to fall forward. At the last moment he put out his hands and saved himself. Blood trickled from his nose and mouth and made small scarlet spots in the dust.

Corby shook his head twice, inhaled deeply and staggered upright, but his hands were limp at his sides and, clearly, he was only half conscious.

Ventnor knew nothing of rules; the word 'sportsmanship' had not been included in his vocabulary so he hit again with all his force. This time Corby went right down and stayed there, breathing stertorously and showing the whites of his eyes.

It was then that several young men appeared from various parts of the village and began to run towards him shouting: "Killer! Rapist! Robber!" Some of them carried heavy sticks or throwing clubs.

Ventnor looked wildly about him, saw his cause was hopeless and turned to run.

Someone threw a stone, grazing his leg and then his

9

reflexes took over and he was running out of the village at full speed.

There were shouts behind him and the sound of pursuit but he did not look back. A stone, probably from a sling, hissed past his head. A throwing club, making a whirring sound, passed above him, struck a bank of earth and bounced high into the air.

He looked upwards, seeking, if possible, a quicker way to high ground and, on a hillock far to his right, he saw a figure. Only later did the significance of what he had seen sink into his mind. Stones were flying about him and his lungs were laboring but there was no mistake—the Padre!

The Padre stood on a hillock, arms folded, feet slightly apart, staring downwards as if in triumph.

A club struck Ventnor's shoulder painfully and then he was round a bend in the path which gave him temporary cover, but he knew that the hunt was far from ended. There were shouts behind him, jeering, hoots of encouragement and, from the cultivation patches, the mocking laughter of the women. God, it must be a thousand paces to the top—he'd never do it!

Somehow, however, his feet still pounded on the rough soil. His vision was blurred and tinged with scarlet and he felt as if there were a knife wound in his side, but he did not falter. It was as if his pain-wracked body labored upwards on its own; as if his own fears and terrors drove it onwards and it was determined not to succumb. Yet it shouted for respite, the lungs burned and throbbed, blood pounded noisily in his head and his legs felt grossly heavy yet curiously numb.

Then, somehow, as if in a dream, he reached the flat rolling land above the village, turned onto the path for Del and staggered to an uncertain stop.

About a thousand paces down the path to Del another group of men stood ready to head him off. All of them were armed and two carried bows.

Ventnor, wheezing for breath, did the only thing possible. He turned and ran in the opposite direction.

There was no path, only the uneven ground and a long slope undulating slowly upwards. He knew why there was no path—he was heading towards forbidden territory and,

10

once he reached the boundary line, he would be in it. He admitted to himself that he was frightened but he was more frightened of the immediate danger.

The first pursuit party which had, no doubt, been joined by Corby, thirsting for vengeance, had reached level ground. A quick glance behind him showed that the second party had also taken up the chase.

Then suddenly there was a second line of stones, this time painted red, and he hurled himself across them. He ran until he was safely out of arrow range then let himself collapse, literally sobbing with relief and exhaustion.

He lay, it seemed, a long time, his heart beating so violently it seemed to thud against his ribs. His lungs ached, his clothing was soaked and sweat trickled down his body in streams. Finally he rolled over and sat upright.

"Del boy!" Corby's voice shouting from a distance but was clearly audible. "Del boy, you think you got away?" The voice paused then went on. "You think you safe now?" A shout of laughter from the others. "You safe all right, Del boy, yes, you safe there but try and get back, jest try."

Another shout of laughter from the others then Corby's voice again. "Maybe you wait for darkness, eh? Won't be no darkness for you, boy, not for you. We light fires on boundary, walk up and down with torches. Try getting back, eh? Just try."

Laughter, a series of jeering and obscene threats then Corby's voice again. "Only one thing to do, Del friend, you come to us and maybe we beat you up only a little or you can just keep going. Yes, you can do that, you can keep going. Know what's lying out there, what chance you'll stand? Know what happens to those who leave?"

Ventnor struggled shakily upright and looked at the group of menacing figures slightly below. Then he turned slowly and walked shakily but steadily in the opposite direction.

On the outskirts of Gret the Padre dispatched a message:

Subject: Ventnor, Robert. Classification 225/9/446.
Characteristic alteration in the identity disc of this specimen indicates increasing G-positive.
Local population therefore incited to "elimination level."

11

Unfortunately, however, specimen escaped by flight beyond the boundaries.

                    Padre 4

                              G.B. S.E. Sector D-14

The message was received and passed through various departments before it ended up in the right office but on the wrong desk.

Hobart tossed it on the right one. "Yours, old man."

Matheson nodded, studied it and frowned. "My God, another 'marker' job. I hate endorsing these things."

Hobart moved his shoulders slightly. "Routine, all it needs is your signature."

"My signature deprives a man of his life."

"Oh, come off it, you know damn well it's necessary."

Matheson sighed, tiredly. "Wish I was so damn certain or, for that matter, so detachedly and insufferably self-righteous."

"Let's not get personal, old chap. You're not being *scientific* about this. One connot mix sentiment with science—history should prove that."

"It does, it does. At the same time, such convictions fail to salve my conscience."

Hobart chuckled dryly. "Don't look now, but your inhibitions are showing." Then, more gently: "Look, its an experimental culture. It is housed, clothed, medically examined and controlled. This culture, if it is to succeed, cannot afford variants. Four generations of psycho-genetic control cannot be done in for the sake of one lousy variant. God, man! All the specimens are well-treated, well-fed, literate, within limitations. All we do is guide."

Matheson shook his head. "Sometimes I wonder—I wonder if it will ever mature. A few hundred thousand villages dotting the coastlines of the world—will they *ever* form the basis of a new and stable civilization?"

Hobart spread his hands. "The cultures inland are not permitted to exist for nothing but for comparison purposes, so let's do a little comparing, eh? What have we got inland? A host of blasted savages that almost go back to the Stone Age. It is true that some possess a few ancient fire-arms but the picture is there for anyone to see. These savages are divided into groups or, more correctly, tribes. These tribes fight wars, hold superstitious rites, and entertain forms of government that go right back to the cave-dweller. Absolute dictatorship under a king or paranoic leader, they employ witch-doctors, medicine men and morally and hygienically they are so many beasts."

Matheson nodded but was still obviously dubious. "This man"—he glanced at the message again—"this man Ventnor is heading for the wild areas—why do I have to endorse his execution? They'll kill him—if not the savages it will be something else. He can't survive."

"Orders are orders, my friend. We make dead sure."

"I suppose so." Matheson nodded then endorsed the order with a peculiar suggestion of savagery. "You're right, everyone is right, nonetheless I cannot escape the feeling that we think we're omnipotent. . . ."

Ventnor walked stiffly onwards. Strangely, for a virtual primitive, he was a realist almost to the point of fatalism. He could add it up on his fingers. If they said they would stop him from going back, they would stop him. If he did not go back, his absence would be reported and his very presence in forbidden territory would ensure his execution.

Ventnor did not want to die but he was fully aware of the fact that he was going to. He was resigned, bitterly resigned; he hadn't *done* anything, not deliberately.

He shrugged. Might as well go on, what difference did it make? He had about three days before they sent a marker—if this hostile territory permitted him to live that long.

Lengthening shadows reminded him that darkness was coming and he realized suddenly that he was tired to the point of exhaustion.

He found a hollow into which twigs, dead leaves and dry grass had drifted and lay down, uncaring if something got him in the night.

When he awoke, just before dawn, his body was stiff and cold but his mind was clearer. He rose, swinging his arms to restore the circulation and relieve the stiffness in his muscles. His body still ached from the previous day's gauntlet but, apart from that, he felt tolerably fit.

13

He looked about him. Slowly rising ground covered in sparse grass, outcroppings of white chalk, a few stunted trees clinging defiantly to the soil and, far to his left, the white dawn-glimmer of the ocean.

He walked stiffly forwards, conscious that he was both hungry and thirsty.

He was fortunate—after a few hundred paces he found a hollow in the soil which was filled with rain water. He drank, uncaring that it was slightly rank and white with chalk.

When he raised his head a few moments later, he was shocked to see a *protage* growing, splendidly alone and fully mature, a bare twenty paces away. Probably grown from a wind-born seed from one of the cultivation patches.

He devoured the juicy green leaves ravenously, pushing them into his mouth with his fingers. Finally, satisfied, he wiped his hands on his shirt-front and stood upright. As he did so, something caught his eye—a curious rectangular object protruding from the soil.

He bent down, puzzled. The object was half covered in moss but there was something about it. He scratched away some of the moss with a sharp stone. The object was white and covered with black symbols which, although curiously unlike the script of villages, was, after some effort, understandable.

The symbols said—although they conveyed no particular significance—*Dover 3 K.L. DEAL*—the rest of the object was broken at the end.

He shrugged uncomprehendingly and went on, wary of danger. This was, he reminded himself, forbidden territory into which he was venturing.

II

DESPITE HIS WARINESS, his mind was active as he tried to recall all he had heard about the territory. He was surprised to discover it was very little and most of it was implication rather than fact. A major part was hearsay, someone who knew someone who had—or more often, repeated the memories of a long dead relative.

14

He flicked open the files of memory trying to separate fact from general acceptance. There had been—so the Masters said—a great war which had ravaged the entire world. Ventnor's education had been psycho-monitored so the word 'war' conveyed very little to him. He had a blurred mental picture of fire and destruction in some vague way engineered by evil men but very little else.

According to general opinion in these ravaged areas—forbidden territories—were beasts, huge never-dying fires, dreadful diseases and invisible creatures which struck one down without warning.

He shivered slightly. He could see no beasts or fires, but disease, like the monsters, was invisible. He went grimly onwards with a fluttery feeling of fear in his stomach.

He reached a rising slope and began to climb it. Half way up, a detecting device embedded in the soil responded to his body heat and immediately recorded a complete picture, height, weight, approximate age, general characteristics and, to make quite sure, a photograph.

The information was transferred inland and a man spoke: "Hello! Looks as though a specimen has escaped from the culture tray. Our friends won't like that."

"Escaped or expelled? They're not particular."

"I know. I often wonder why they bother. They'll kill him before he gets far anyway."

"My guess is that they like to make sure irrespective of the fact that his chances of survival are ninety-five to one against. They like to stick to the book—'deviants must be liquidated regardless'."

"You're probably right. Poor devil, I wonder if he's intelligent enough to realize— Oh, hell, keep an eye on him anyway, Roger, perhaps he'll get near enough for us to help him."

Roger said, "Sure"—and added pessimistically—"they never do, you know. Our friends will burn him down within three days at the latest." He paused, frowning. "Haven't we a patrol out somewhere around there?"

"Twenty kilometers away. We can try them but I don't think they'll make it in time. In the first place it's a damned dangerous area and, in the second, he's still in Hubel's Kingdom."

15

"Think I'll try anyway, if only to spite our friends on the Island. In my considered opinion, they not only think they own the world but played a major part in its creation which, in view of history, is not a myth to be encouraged. . . ."

Ventor strode on but with increasing caution. Half an hour later he found a length of substance which he thought was metal and weighed it experimentally in his hand. It was clumsy but would serve as a useful club in the event of trouble. It increased his confidence without affecting his wariness.

He came to the top of a slight rise, make-shift club swinging loosely in his hand, and stopped dead, his mouth opening foolishly in disbelief.

Below him the land sloped steeply downwards to a wide valley and the sea. It was the valley which stunned him for, completely filling it, was the ruins of a city, so vast, it staggered his imagination.

Ventnor was used to villages which seldom contained more than eight hundred inhabitants. The concept of a community of forty or fifty times that number had never entered his mind.

He looked about him again, conscious of a need for reassurance, but he could find none.

To his left, a huge pile of rubble, still vaguely resembling a building, topped a steep hill. Below him the ruins of the city remained unchanged.

He saw that most of the streets were overgrown with weeds, that the few buildings which remained were shells and that, generally, all that remained were the outlines of foundations. Yet from this height, despite the rubble and weed, the order of the city was clearly seen.

Great highways, as wide as the village of Del, converged upon what had clearly been a double harbor. Now only a few blackened projections, like the fangs of a reef, protruded above the calm blue water. Within, twisted hulks, suggesting ocean-going vessesls, were still visible beneath the surface.

Despite his awe, he was conscious of a curious melancholy. It was dead, it was like looking at the skeleton of a long-

16

remembered friend without knowing how or when he had died.

Despite this, the city drew him; he was frightened yet fascinated. Almost against his will and gripping his club tightly, he began the long descent to the ruins below.

After a few hundred paces he stumbled and realized that he was walking on the broken, weed-covered surface of what had once been a major highway. He followed it downwards, frightened, often stumbling but now determined to go on.

As he descended, the resemblance to an orderly city slowly faded. There were only low walls and moss-covered foundations. The streets were choked with weeds, stunted trees and a bewildering tangle of ivy.

Despite the bright sunshine, the city conveyed a frightening sense of desolation and despair. Here, he thought uneasily, invisible monsters might dwell unchallenged.

As he reached level ground a solitary brown bird flew out of the tangle ahead of him so suddenly he raised his club in self-defence. He was conscious that his skin felt tight and his breathing shallow and jerky.

"I'm frightened," he thought and experienced a brief moment of panic. Having got down here, he wanted nothing better than to get away. Away from the desolation, the whisper of wind and the rustle of leaves.

He looked back. The hill he had descended now looked vast and impossible of ascent. The heap of rubble at the summit seemed to him now dark and vaguely menacing.

He hurried forward seeking his way out of the city which had become a maze—a maze which almost dictated his path. Here and there, streets were so choked with weed and rubble that progress was impossible.

With the hill he had descended on his right and the sea behind him he found himself heading inland again.

He took the remains of the *protage* from his pocket and began to eat as he walked.

He came to a narrow chalky stream, forded it cautiously and climbing the opposite bank, stopped abruptly.

Slightly ahead of him was a wide shallow depression—the word 'crater' had not been included in his vocabulary and he thought of it simply as a hole. From the 'hole' came a curious and somehow threatening hissing sound.

17

Warily, crouching more from instinct that experience, the club held tightly in his hand, he crept forwards.

The first thing he saw was the man. He stood with his back to a low wall in attitude both of desperation and defiance. He held a length of polished metal in his hand which flashed brightly as it caught the sun but he held it weakly as if on the point of exhaustion.

Ventnor saw the reason. The man's garments hung about his body in bloody tatters. The half naked chest was criss-crossed with long parallel scratches which were bleeding profusely. Occasionally the bright metal thing in the man's hand drooped from weariness, touched the ground but was jerked back into the guard position with obvious effort.

Ventnor edged forward a few more inches and almost instantly 'froze' with a cold feeling in his stomach.

About twenty feet from the man in an uneven but menacing arc were six 'things'. It was some seconds before he was able to relate the 'things' to something familiar and then it came to him—cats!

He had often seen wild cats beyond the villages but these! They bore the shape of cats but there the resemblance ended. The head was flatter and wider, the fangs longer and unpleasantly curved. The claws, too, were like gray curved knives, apparently did not retract and appeared to grip the ground like sharp unbending fingers.

It was their general appearance, however, which appalled him most—the creatures were furless. The skin was a dull blotchy gray and as smooth as plastic. It made them look sly, vicious and, in some inexplicable way, obscene.

They watched the man unblinkingly, flat naked heads close to the ground and, periodically, as if following some precise plan, one or other of the creatures would arch its back, straighten its legs and hiss like a spitting kettle.

Ventnor, stiff with terror, saw one of the creatures at the far end of the arc suddenly race forward on stiff legs and leap. The speed with which it moved was incredible.

The bright metal weapon swung in a glittering arc—too late. The creature was back to its original position long before the defensive blow had completed its sweep but, on the man's naked forearm, another line of deep scratches began to ooze scarlet.

Ventnor was not sufficiently literate to put mental words to what he saw but inwardly, deep in his mind, he understood. These creatures were semi-intelligent and were working to a precise plan. They went in, clawed, and were gone before the man could defend himself for, despite his weapon, they were too fast for him. In due course, sheer exhaustion and loss of blood would bring the man to his knees and then the whole pack would move in as a single unit and claw him to pieces.

Ventnor glanced cautiously over his shoulder, wondering if he could creep back unnoticed. The rubble over which he had crawled, however, looked heaped and singularly precarious. He'd never get back without making a noise.

He looked again at the man, weapon still clutched desperately in his hand, and was suddenly conscious of a curious and unfamiliar compassion. Alone, the man hadn't a chance—not a chance. A sense of rightness, of responsibility began to assert itself in Ventnor's mind despite his natural terror.

He hesitated, undecided, moved slightly and, beneath his left elbow, a huge piece of rubble moved slightly as if balanced on something beneath.

It was the movement which gave him the idea. Cautiously, and with agonizing slowness, he assumed a crouching position, bent forward and grasped the piece of rubble with both hands.

It seemed to him that his muscles cracked with enough noise to be heard several feet away. Nonetheless, somehow he straightened, somehow, sweat trickling down his face and the blood pounding in his ears, he raised the object above his head.

Briefly he glanced at the hole, at the exhausted man and then with a grunt of effort, pitched his burden at one of the cat-things directly below him. He had no idea how much his bomb weighed, but it looked and felt heavy enough. Before it landed, the club was back in his left hand and he was throwing a big round stone with his right.

The cat-thing below apparently possessed acute senses for, at the last moment it darted forward but just a fraction too late. The heavy stone caught its hind quarters, pinning it to the ground and it screamed shrilly, front claws scrabbling desperately at the soil.

The heavy stone Ventnor had thrown hit one of the creatures in the side, knocking it over. It rolled over twice, spitting and clawing at the air and then it was on its feet again. It spun round, curved fangs bared, looking for its attacker.

It was then that the man took four swift paces forward and swung his weapon in a vicious arc.

Suddenly there seemed to be two cats and then Ventnor realised that the bright weapon had cut the creature completely in half. Seizing the advantage of surprise, he jumped the ten feet to the bottom of the hole and swung his club with all his strength.

There was a curiously satisfying crunching sound and there was a limp gray thing, twitching but lifeless in front of him.

The rest of the creatures, apparently afraid, suddenly dove in all directions and went bounding away over the rubble like frightened race horses.

The man with the weapon walked unsteadily over to the lump of rubble Ventnor had thrown and stabbed downwards. The clawing spitting thing which had been pinned to the ground was suddenly silent.

The man tottered back to the wall and leaned against it, panting. "Take a lot of killing them gouge-cats." He extended a bloody hand. "Dunno who you are, mate, but thanks. Took a lot of nerve; they could have turned on you easily." He gripped Ventnor's hand with obvious sincerity. "Yeah, could have turned on you, see? You caught 'em by surprise. They don't like surprise, undermines 'em, surprise does."

He thrust his long bright weapon into a container dangling from his waist. "Let's get out of here. I'll wash in the stream up ahead—come on." He went unsteadily but determinedly forward, tattered, dusty, the blood-soaked trousers fluttering in threads about his legs.

After a few hundred paces they came to a continuation of the chalky stream. It was only a few inches deep but the man removed his clothes, lay full length and let the water run over him.

20

"Name is Berman," he remarked from the water. "Joe Berman."

Ventnor felt called upon to reply and gave his own name.

The other sat upright, eyes narrowed. "You're from one of the villages, should have seen it, no one dresses like that here—what you doing in Hubel's Kingdom?"

"They drove me out." Ventnor went into details.

The other stood upright. "I'm still listening." He pointed. "See my belt? Little bag tied on it, inside you'll find a little pot full of green stuff. Chuck it over."

Ventnor found the object near the weapon-holder and tossed it over.

Berman caught it deftly, unscrewed the top and began to smear his wounds with the greenish substance it contained.

"A-septic this is, see? Gouge-cats is poison, you got to clean it out." He winced and grinned twistedly. "Burns but cleans, see?" He screwed the top on the jar, fetched his tattered clothing from the side of the stream and dropped it into the water. "Blood, got to get rid of the stink of it. Everything that crawls will be after us otherwise."

He trod on the soaked garments, wrung them out carefully then spread them on the bank of the stream. "Soon dry in the sun." He paused, frowning. "You understand I should kill you? Hubel doesn't like strangers, Hubel doesn't. Not to worry, you saved my life. You good brave boy and I'll put in a word. I'm a lieuty, reccy lieuty, first class. Hubel listens to his officers, you'll be all right, I'll see to that. In any case, Hubel likes brave boys, maybe make you a soldier, eh?"

He became suddenly conscious of Ventnor's blank uncomprehending face and grinned. "You ain't got a clue what I'm jawing about, can see that. Don't teach much in the villages I'm told. Never mind, let's get moving 'fore them cats get their nerve back." He sighed and looked at his wounds. "Should have known better than to take a short cut but its usually fairly safe in the day."

He felt his clothing. "Dry enough. Once we get clear of the city the cats won't bother. Cats don't like the open, cats don't."

21

A few moments later they were moving on but, after about a thousand paces, Berman turned.

"Disc! You got a disc, boy, you got a disc?"

"Why yes, I've—"

Berman ripped open his shirt before he could finish the sentence.

"As I thought, like the one the gel had. Gotta get rid of it. Metal's tough but brittle, needs a sharp hard knock. Put the chain across that big flat stone there."

"But I was told never to—"

"You're out now, got to lose it, see? Don't know quite what they do or how they do it but disc burns up suddenly, you burn with it, follow?" He found a heavy stone and weighed it in his hand. "Mind your face—ah—again—got him!"

There was a tinkling sound and Ventnor watched the disc and chain fall to the ground with something akin to superstitious terror.

"Come." Berman tugged at his arm. "You're safe now. There's a rest cave at the top of the hill, we'll bed up there."

They followed what had clearly been a road. It went up and down, over low hills and down into small valleys. Finally it began to ascend steadily.

Later, far behind them, when the afternoon sun was beginning to sink towards the horizon, an identity disc suddenly flickered, turned white and puffed upwards in a sheet of flame.

The disc was 'tuned' to an instrument far out in the Atlantic and the chemical content of the minor explosion analyzed. The readings showed no chemical contents such as might be expected from the destruction of the organic human body and, almost immediately, alarms began to ring.

Hobart looked at the readings and turned pale. "My God, Matheson, he's escaped! This will mean an investigation, heads are going to roll before this business is finished."

At the same time, inland, another group of men had already received orders to pick Ventnor up.

There were six in the patrol but it did not look like a patrol. It looked, as it was intended to, like a hunting party. The men were bearded, their clothing tattered and make-shift and their limbs, although bronzed had been artificially stained to suggest ingrained dirt.

All the men carried weapons, most of them knives and clumsy-looking cross-bows.

The leader, however, carried a short cutting spear which, after a cautious look round, he pushed point first into the soil.

"Patrol G for George," he said to the end of the spear.

He waited and the spear spoke: "Receiving you, George—map reference, please."

The leader gave it and the spear said: "Hum, you won't intercept our bird from there."

"Where is he?"

"Around fourteen stroke five or, to save you looking it up, just leaving what used to be Lydden. I'm very much afraid you'll have to trek to Hubel's Kingdom and make peace signs."

"Thanks for nothing. They don't always recognize them."

"Peary, we want this man badly. Not only is he a specimen but he's shed his disc. If necessary trade your top goods, blind King Hubel with science, but get him!"

"Will try—out." Peary pulled the spear out of the ground and grinned twistedly. "We've got a mission, boys— Hubel's Kingdom."

"The specimen—is he that important?"

"Genetically and biologically I suppose he is."

"You hope he is." Puttick was scowling. "This patrol always gets the dirt."

"And that bloody great hill," said one of his companions, sourly. "Why do we always have to be near Charing?"

They looked upwards.

Charing Hill was not a big hill, not really a steep climb, but years ago there had been a lot of fighting on those slopes. Time had wiped away the scars of battle, stunted trees and coarse grass covered the churned soil, but other things remained. There were still snap-traps, chase-mines and micro-cannons. True, there was a safe path but it wound up and down and in and out until you thought it was never going to end. There were also creatures, the creatures were quite harmless but repulsive. In short, they made you sick to look at them. . . .

23

III

IT WAS TWILIGHT when Ventnor and his companion reached the top of the long winding hill. Berman, obviously exhausted and weak from loss of blood had to stop frequently to rest.

Finally he said: "Thank God—this way."

There was a round hole in a grassy bank and they crawled into it. Inside it was still another hole, but wider and deeper. The earth walls were held from collapse by some ancient tree trunks and some plastic boarding.

In the fading light Ventnor saw that it contained a large bin of tubers and a tub of reasonably clean drinking water. Beyond were two straw-filled palliasses.

Herman drank greedily of the water, helped himself to three or four tubers and crawled to the nearest palliasse. "God, I'm gowed! Sleep for a hundred years."

Ventnor, drank, ate three tubers and lay down himself. But before he could relax, the earth jerked and shivered beneath him.

He sat bolt upright. "What was that!"

"What?" Berman sounded half asleep.

"The ground shook."

"Oh—yeah—yeah. You don't know, do you? Not to worry —one of the repeaters. Elham Valley or Barham."

"Repeaters?"

"Oh, brother! Look, we'll pass one tomorrow, tell—about it—then—" Berman's voice trailed away and he began to snore.

Strangely it was Ventnor who had to be wakened at dawn.

"Come on, boy, rouse up. It's daylight."

As they left the artificial cave, the ground shook again but Berman made no comment.

They walked steadily, if windingly along level ground and Ventnor, glancing back, could just glimpse the pile of ruin on the hilltop which he had passed the day before.

"What was that place?" He pointed.

24

"Them ruins? Sage says it used to be a castle—sort of fort—story is that the Indoes made a last stand there."

"Castle? Indoes?"

"Oh Gawd! Forget it, will you."

"Who is Sage?"

"Oh Gawd twice over! Sage is our wise-man—can you follow that?"

"Yes, that I understand."

"I'll chalk it up and you leave it, eh? We've a long way to go."

They came to a half-dead tree, leaning sideways curiously, its upper branches torn and blackened.

Berman made a gesture. "We turn off here, skirt round. If there's a flash, drop fast."

"I don't understand you."

"How do you get by in the villages? Listen, if I shout drop flat, you throw yourself down as fast as you can—clear?"

"Clear."

"Come on then." He led the way at right angles to the road they had been following. It led across churned and blackened soil. Pale-looking grass, moss and a profusion of sickly-looking white toadstools existed in sunken hollows but on level ground it looked as if the vegetation had been burned away.

Suddenly the bright rising sun seemed to flicker curiously and Berman shouted: "Drop!"

Ventnor, already 'on edge' flung himself full length so heavily that he hurt his ribs. As he did so a searing blue-green light seemed to fill his eyes and there was an ear-splitting noise like the slamming of a gigantic door. There was a gust of burning air which rushed above him and a hail of fragments peppered his body. Something huge and heavy struck the ground a bare forty paces away.

Berman rolled over, sat upright and brushed dust, twigs and lumps of blackened soil from his clothing.

"All right, you can get up now but watch it. We could be safe for hours or it could blow again in the next thirty paces. They can't be timed and they don't give no warning, repeaters don't."

Ventnor stood cautiously upright. "What was it?"

"There you got me, boy. Blows every so often, sometimes

25

twice a day, sometimes twenty. Sage says the Indoes put them there to stop the Engineers, there's another in the Elham valley. Didn't do them no good, I hear, the Engineers came up the coast at night in a fleet of boats and took them in the rear."

Ventnor shook his head. The words 'Indoes' and 'Engineers' were meaningless to him, but he was beginning to get the drift. "Then the Indoes hid in the castle?"

"More or less, boy. They made their last stand there but the Engineers blew it down on their heads."

"What was it all about; what did they do it for?"

"I'm a soldier, I wouldn't know. Lot of tales about this and that. See Sage when you're settled in. Sage knows it all and Sage likes to talk, Sage does. Job to stop once he gets going."

Gradually they left the blackened area behind them and then, far ahead, on the top of the low hill, there was a series of bright flashes.

"Hello, they've seen us." Berman sounded pleased. "Signal flashes they are. Won't be long now before we meet a patrol."

He was right. Less than twenty minutes later, three bearded men suddenly rose from a hollow at the side of the broken road. All carried bows and the leader held a slender lance.

"Who goes?"

"Reccy Lieuty Berman."

"Password."

"*Dawn.*"

"You're a day out of date, Lieuty. Lucky I know you by sight—who is the intruder?"

"Village boy. Saved me skin, he did." Berman went into long and elaborate details.

The others listened, looking curiously and somewhat doubtfully at Ventnor.

When he had finished, the leader nodded. "Better send a message—tell 'em you're coming." He held up his hand and the small mirror he held flickered briefly.

From a low hill some distance away came an answering flash. "Right, he's receiving." The patrol leader made a motion with the lance. "Right, pass friends."

26

They walked on, apparently by themselves, but Ventnor had the uncomfortable feeling that they were surrounded and under constant observation.

Just after noon they climbed a long hill, descended slowly, climbed again and, at the summit, Ventnor, staring ahead, came to an abrupt halt.

At first he had to convince himself that what he saw was a building and not, as he had at first supposed, a peculiarly shaped hill. He had never seen anything but a single floored hut and the structure he was looking at dazed him. It seemed to reach the sky and—he could find no suitable words for the building, but it stirred him strangely both by its beauty and its immensity. The tall spires against the pale blue of the afternoon sky filled him with superstitious awe and unfamiliar humility.

"Come on." Berman tugged at his arm. "What's up?"

"That—that huge hut—what is it?"

"Hut—hut? Oh, my Gawd!" Berman suddenly burst out laughing. "That ain't no hut, boy, that's the Feederal."

"Feederal? I don't understand."

"It's just the Feederal, mate, Canterbury Feederal. Only building standing in the Kingdom, the only old building that is. Reckon it was left alone because it's haunted."

"What is 'haunted'?"

"Can't tell you proper. ı.'s just that behind the walls things drift around, things which ain't got no body. They're there but you can see right through 'em, like mist they are. Cold winds rush at you from nowhere on a sweating hot day and sometimes you can hear people singing, sad like, a long way away."

He shivered. "Come on! Hubel doesn't like waiting, Hubel doesn't."

They went on and finally came to a huge and broken wall. Beneath it and stretching away into the distance were rows of crude huts. The slender spires of what Berman called the Feederal seemed to look down on them sadly and almost with compassion.

An armed escort emerged from the hutments and conducted them back.

"When we meet the King, let me do the talking." Berman sounded confident. "Oh, and yeah, when he speaks to you, you call him Sire, got that? Ah, there he is—"

Only many months later did Ventnor realize that the self-styled king was something of a character with a unique if primitive philosophy.

At first sight, Hubel was anything but prepossessing. Hubel had once seen a picture of a clean-shaven man and had been trying ever since to acquire a similar smoothness of face. As all he possessed to achieve it was an ancient pair of scissors, he wore a hacked and uneven black stubble.

He had little black eyes, a flattened kind of nose and thick red lips. He looked ferocious but laughed frequently.

King Hubel, despite the summer heat, wore a 1917 tin hat, shorts, two singlets, and a thick plastic raincoat. Slung over his shoulder by a strap was, Ventnor learned later, a highly polished Ross rifle, vintage nineteen hundred.

Hubel listened attentively while Berman, with a great deal of gesticulation, described the events leading up to their arrival.

When he had finished, Hubel made an imperious gesture with his hand. "Come here, you."

"Sire?" Ventnor had decided that it would be wise to be respectful from the start.

Hubel looked vaguely flattered. "Nice! Lieuty gave him the right line 'fore he got here; means he can learn too."

He looked Ventnor up and down, if not with friendliness at least without hostility. Hubel had strong reasons for disliking the villages. Years ago he had tried to take one and had lost forty-three men. Not that the villagers had done anything but run as soon as his war party had appeared but a curtain of fire had appeared between them as they ran. The fire-curtain had advanced towards them like a rain-belt. Hubel could still see some of his best soldiers puffing up in mist when it touched them.

For months after that, his patrols had been picked off and harassed by great flying black tubes. Things that came whispering out of the sky when no one was looking. Hubel knew a show of force when he saw it. Since then he had left the villages severely alone.

"So you was chucked out?" he said.

"Yes, Sire."

28

"Hum, well, Lieuty Berman tells me you're a good brave boy. Berman's one of my men and you saved him so that's good enough for me. Tell you what, how'd you like to be one of my soldiers?"

Ventnor had no idea what a soldier was but Hubel's next words made it plain.

"You'll serve me, see? You'll be taught to use a bow, a knife an' things like that. Then, if I tell you to fight, you'll fight, see? If you fight good, learn good, maybe I'll make you a Sarnt or even a Lieuty like Berman here. Wait—" He placed two fingers in his mouth and produced a piercing whistle.

The armed bearded men surrounding King Hubel parted to make way for a number of girls and young women.

"Look· 'em over, village boy. If I make you a Sarnt, you can pick out two for yourself—providing they ain't mine at the time o' course."

Ventor looked them over uneasily. Several of them were personable but none of them were particularly clean. Here, apparently, there were no standards of personal cleanliness such as were insisted upon in the villages.

The girls looked at him with interest and giggled.

He said, guardedly, "Thank you, Sire."

"Think nothing of it. I treat my soldiers well, I do. You ask around, boy, you'll find out. On top of that you get free food, a bed and weapons. What could be fairer than that?"

He paused and looked at the other thoughtfully. "Berman tells me you don't know much, gotta lot to learn like. Well, fine, but listen here, what counts most in this world is staying alive. Maybe you don't know what the Indoes were or what a repeater is but if you have to fight a chap what does and he knows less about staying alive than you, you're going to come out on top. Survival that's what. First thing is knowing how to survive. If you don't know that, what good is learning to you? They'll bury you pretty quick, that's what'll happen, you and your learning—"

He was interrupted by a thin teenage youth who suddenly appeared at his side slightly out of breath.

"Well, messenger, what is it?"

"Message from Sarnt of signal post three, Sire." The youth

29

closed his eyes obviously intent on repeating the exact words. "Sarnt says to tell you—six Maidstone boys entering territory with peace signs."

"Maidstone boys, eh?" Hubel frowned. "Wonder what they want, must be something very special. They don't come this way for nothing them boys don't." He scratched the stubble of his cheek in deep thought. "Better tell the Sarnt to signal ahead and find out what they want, tell him to give 'em safe passage until he finds out."

"Yes, Sire." The youth raced away.

Hubel stared after him lost in thought. The Maidstone boys troubled him in a way he could not quite explain even to himself. He'd fought and conquered six minor kingdoms in his life but when he'd tried the Maidstone area he'd run into big trouble and his men had taken the biggest beating of their lives. The Maidstone boys didn't stand up and fight like normal people. The first line of attack had run into the withering fire of massed cross-bows from skilled marksmen concealed in the most unlikely places. His men had gone down in dozens.

The next attacking wave had suffered even worse. This one had run into crossfire from more crossbows which had not revealed their presence in the first attack.

Realizing he was beaten, he had organized a fighting retreat but the Maidstone boys had not exploited their success. Instead voices had shouted warnings and advice.

"Don't try it again, Hubel, or we'll wipe you out to a man."

"You leave us alone and we'll leave you alone."

Hubel was a realist and knew what he would have done in their position. He would have followed up and taken over the entire Kingdom. To this day he still didn't understand why they hadn't. Instead, they'd been content to maintain their borders and respect his—it didn't make sense.

Stranger still, after the battle, instead of disposing swiftly and mercifully of the wounded, they'd picked them up and treated them. Then, once recovered, they'd been escorted politely to the border and *released*.

Hubel scowled inwardly. True they didn't stand up and fight in a straight battle but if you managed to get hold of one it was no joke. He remembered a five-man patrol

30

limping in with one dead and three badly injured. The five had seen a single Maidstone boy alone, hidden themselves and jumped him. One had a broken arm, another dragged his leg, the rest, apart from the dead man, had torn muscles.

The patrol had been executed for incompetence, of course, until further incidents had convinced him that these Maidstone boys were more than a match for any of his men in a straight fight.

They had a thing called 'unarmed combat' which, apparently gave them powers above the normal. Hubel was both enraged yet awed by their efficiency.

His thoughts were interrupted by the return of the messenger.

"Sarnt says, Sire, the Maidstone boys want to talk with you. They say they want to trade."

"Trade?" Hubel scowled. "What would they want to trade?"

He decided there was a catch somewhere but it would be wise if he let them through and waited to find out.

"Tell Sarnt to give them safe passage," he said. "But tell him to double the strength of every guard post all along the route—right, get moving."

He became aware of Ventnor again. "All right, lad, that's all. You run along with Berman here and he'll show you the cookhouse and a place to sleep."

Berman jerked his head. "This way."

Ventnor followed him obediently but was studying his surroundings curiously.

Canterbury, apart from the 'feederal' and the broken wall, was very much like the city by the sea. The piles of stone were more numerous but it had the same moss-covered foundations and heaps of rubble. True there were numerous pathways through the weed-choked streets and, here and there, half-hearted attempts had been made to clear the streets completely. Generally, however, the impression was the same—the skeleton of something long dead.

Berman stopped by a long, lop-sided hut composed of wood and plastic boarding. "Hi! Cooks! Field patrol for food."

He squatted down on the ground and, after a minute or so, two elderly women brought out a round metal con-

31

tainer in which was a steaming brown liquid. The container had the words Tractor Fuel in faded white lettering on its side but the words were meaningless to both of them.

They were presented with metal plates and a plastic spoon.

Berman dipped in his spoon and ladled the substance onto his plate. In it were lumps of some solid substance.

Ventnor, normally, would have been wary of such a diet, but already he was experiencing the pangs of hunger. The food, although greasy, was nourishing and he ate greedily. Fortunately, for his peace of mind, he was unaware he was eating a stew of *protage*, wild dog and an unfortunate crow—the victim of a small boy with a sling.

When Berman had finished, he lay down where he was and immediately fell asleep. Ventnor found a heap of straw nearby and immediately collapsed.

Both men were awakened in the early evening by shouts and running feet.

"The Maidstone boys—the Maidstone boys are coming!"

Hubel was ready for them. He sat on an ancient gas drum inwardly uneasy but outwardly calm.

Behind him was his elite guard—twelve bearded men with ancient Ross rifles. Behind these was a line of fifty bowmen and, to support it, a double line of spears.

The Maidstone boys were conducted to him with an armed escort and brought to a halt about ten feet away.

One of them took a single pace forward, hands extended in a peace sign.

"I am Peary," he said. "I am the leader."

Hubel scowled at him. "What you want with me?"

Peary did not answer the question directly but took something from a plastic bag carried by one of the other men.

"Sire, I have here a pair of binoculars. They are very powerful, you may have them."

" 'Noculars!" Hubel's eyes glistened briefly—he owned a blurred and cracked pair of opera glasses of which he was exceedingly proud.

"Try them." Peary held them out and explained to Hubel how to use them.

He spent ten minutes testing them delightedly then scowled again. "What you want?"

Again Peary evaded a direct answer and beckoned Puttick forward. "Look at this man. As you see, he has no hair on his face."

He removed another object from the bag, beckoned one of his men forward and shaved off part of his beard. "Would you like a smooth face, Sire? See how easy this is to use. Just keep pressing this little lever at the side so—"

Hubel was already licking his lips, he was sold and knew it. "What you want?"

Peary smiled. "We want your village boy," he said.

IV

WHILE THESE EVENTS were taking place on land, far out in the Atlantic a none too friendly discussion was taking place concerning them.

They were taking place on an island which was completely artificial. The island had once been a minor weather station anchored to the ocean bed by magno-beams.

With the coming of weather control, however, the island had become obsolete and had been acquired by a private buyer—an industrial concern which went bankrupt in three months.

The white-elephant was then snapped up by a far-seeing magnate who imported a number of experts to make his retreat self-supporting.

When the writing on the wall became even more apparent, the magnate extended his invitation to even more specialists. A large number accepted the invitation, and the island, together with its accommodation, had to be extended to house them.

As civilization began to slide towards collapse, the invitations, although increased, became selective. Only scientists with exceedingly high qualifications or men of learning with an almost unobtainable intelligence quota were invited.

The response to what was now a veritable haven of safety was immediate and represented ninety per cent of the world's best brains.

By this time, the accommodation facilities and the total

area of the island had been doubled several times over. It now contained workshops, extensive laboratories, recreation rooms and places of entertainment.

By this time the magnate was in his dotage and the magagement and up-keep of the island were taken over by a committee.

Five years before the world slid to ruin, however, Megellon arrived.

Arnold Megellon was a dark, dour man with a savage mouth, incredible energy and immense intensity of purpose. He knew, or thought he knew, exactly what was wanted both then and in the future and intended to get it.

He was dedicated, single minded and quite ruthless. There were a large number of 'accidents' and a disquieting number of bodies were consigned to the sea in the course of reorganization. When he had finished, however, the island was a highly efficient functioning unit. Furthermore, it was heavily armed and when, with the coming of chaos, several attempts were made to take it, Arnold's preparations saved it from complete destruction.

It was these attacks which proved Arnold's theories and swung general opinion in his favor. When the combined fleets of three nations attempted to take and hold the island, Arnold's foresight defeated them.

The massive and highly advanced defenses upon which he had insisted and finally forced through the committee, proved to be the island's salvation.

The flagship of the attacking fleet, the contents of its ammunition hold, brought to combustion point by some of the island's advanced equipment, blew skywards with such a titantic explosion that it took three escorting destroyers with it.

The entire engagement lasted exactly twenty minutes, by which time the strike force had lost forty per cent of its effectiveness.

The few missiles which the fleet had managed to release had been successfully picked up and 'about-turned' by deflector beams. Some of these fell among the retreating fleets accounting for another fourteen vessels.

The collapsing governments, faced with failing supplies, riots and economic chaos were incapable of mounting another

34

attack. They did, however, play their last card. It was more a gesture of revenge than anything else. They released a hail of missiles and mounted the most massive air armada the world had ever seen.

The missiles were deflected or turned back so that they exploded in or above the nations from which they had been released.

The air armada was blasted out of the sky long before it was in sight of the island—technically Arnold was now master of the world.

On the Island, of course, he was regarded as a hero. They called him 'leader,' 'saviour' and, subsequently, the 'architect of the future.'

Megellon had ideas. He knew, or thought he knew, the reason the society of the world had failed. He wrote a long, superficially convincing, paper called *Psycho-Sociological Weaknesses and their Cure*, which later became a basis for island policy. He followed this, a year later with: *The Stable Society*. In this work, he revealed his plans for the foundation and creation of a new society—a society made stable by applied psychiatry and genetic manipulation.

He then sat back to wait, but it was not a long vigil. All over the world nations, principalities and powers had ceased to exist. The Island watched as famine, chaos and disease strode across continents and islands. It watched the Indoes, the Engineers, the Tychs and Techs, the Haves and Have-nots, fight their bloody and abortive battles.

When nothing was left, when society was reduced to a few roving, half-starved bands of vagrants, then the Island moved in, selecting and removing the children of the survivors. Experimental villages were set up on the coast lines of the world and the great experiment began. Arnold Megellon was going to build a stable society from the remnants of the old. Like many fanatics and rulers before him, Arnold found a villain—the villain was the Gadgeteer!

The Gadgeteer was, broadly speaking, defined as the sort of imbecile who would take the pin out of a hand grenade to see what happened.

In truth, there was much to support Arnold's theory but, like most single minded men, he produced facts to fit theory and omitted to build a theory from facts.

35

Now, several decades after his sudden death from heart failure, the Island was still rigidly following his policies. The genetic manipulation of the new race could not be undertaken in a day but would require many generations. The work had begun and would continue.

By this time, the Island itself had been extended and increased in area so many times it was virtually a minor continent. Its mass was such that it affected tidal currents to such an extent that it produced climatic changes in various parts of the world. It had roads, traffic, public parks, green belts, lakes, swimming pools and an air service.

In one of the buildings on the Island an intense discussion was taking place with Skeld, the district chief, conducting proceedings.

"In the circumstances, Matheson, I cannot regard you as completely responsible, although the delay in endorsing this order will be entered on the debit side of your record."

"Our primary concern, gentlemen, is to establish the potential of this specimen—well, Matnick?"

Matnick shook his mane of graying hair. "I cannot think of a less dangerous specimen I'd care to see roaming around loose."

"Be specific, please."

"Well, sir, as you are probably aware, genetically, in the process of suppressing a characteristic that same characteristic is, by some peculiar reactionary process, apt to become over-predominant. In two or three generations, of course, we can reduce this tendency but in this specimen the tendency is, shall we say, abnormal. This man Ventnor is, by any standard and in any age, an inventive genius plus. Worse, his sexual urges are likewise over-predominant and, should he form an association with any of these primitive women, he will undoubtedly pass these tendencies on. In which case, of course, we should be compelled to wipe out every primitive in the South East as a safety measure."

"We need those primitives for anthropological studies and comparison purposes," said Seymour sharply.

"I am aware of that, hence the need for haste." He turned. "Have you found him yet, Kimber?"

"Not yet, sir. We tracked him to Bridge and lost him."

36

"How did you lose him?" Skeld's voice was accusing.

"Not my fault, sir. I was using a micro-robotic disguised as a fly—some bloody fool of a primitive swatted it."

"Hum, that means that one of the tribes have him—who runs that area, Holland?"

Holland opened one of his innumerable files. "Could be Hubel or a faction known locally as the Maidstone boys, sir."

"I'd like an outline on these tribes. If we have to go in and get him I'd like to know what we're up against."

Holland did a quick switch with the files. "Hubel—chieftain-type monarch—"

"Never mind the full reading—numbers and strength, please."

"Very well, sir. Hubel has a tribe of roughly thirty thousand and runs an army of about eight thousand. These are primarily general soldiers but include eight hundred bowman. Unfortunately he also possesses twenty-two Ross rifles and three thousand rounds of ammunition. Twelve of the rifles are serviceable and he has an elite guard trained to use them."

"You keep a tight check." Skeld nodded approvingly. "Now these—er—Maidstone boys, please."

"Different story altogether, sir. This is a tribe run by a primitive but highly efficient junta, the whole tribe conforming to strict training rather like the ancient Spartans. These boys have got hold of a military training book somewhere and a manual on unarmed combat. They employ both very effectively. Every man has commando training and, in combat they're pretty formidable. They have no fire-arms but they go in for cross-bows in a big way."

Skeld nodded. "Right, nothing to worry about there. We could use a seeker-missile but, in this case, I'd like to be sure, very sure. We'll send an expert, that way we can get confirmation that the job is done. . . ."

"Excuse me, sir." Kimber's voice was excited. "I've got him."

"You have—where?"

"Passing through an area which used to be called Challock, sir. I assume the Maidstone boys have him. . . ."

In a long past period when a large number of scientists

had been running for the safety of the Island, not all went. Some of the best, including an extraordinary high number of medical people, remained behind. They were dedicated men, without illusions, but determined to do their best where it was most needed.

They, too, had seen the writing on the wall. They, too, made preparations. In every land, in every nation, they formed survival cells by which, they hoped to build society anew.

When chaos finally engulfed the world many of the cells were swept away, but a hard core remained and had, over a period of many years, constructed a highly efficient organization.

They knew, of course, about the Island and its policies. They knew, without being told, that if the Island ever got wind of their presence it would take punitive elimination measures.

The organization, therefore with singular skill and particular attention to detail, disappeared—it became a number of primitive tribes with nothing, outwardly, to distinguish them from others.

It was six men of one of these 'primitive tribes', descendants of the original dedicated scientists who had stayed behind in the times of terror, who were now conducting Ventnor through the ruined village of Challock.

Puttick, bringing up the rear, said, casually: "Hell of a lot of flies around here today."

Peary, who was getting readings on three of the 'flies' said: "Yeah," and put his thumb down in confirmation.

Puttick knew exactly what he meant and for the first time was glad he was going down Charing Hill. They were things among those trees which would eat first and worry about indigestion afterwards. A micro-robotic spy unit disguised as a fly would be useless in the revolting digestive organs of a 'thing'.

Ventnor, for his part, was both bewildered and suspicious. He was fully alive to the fact that he had been traded for a pair of binoculars and a thing which shaved faces, but why? What was so important about *him*?

So far he had spent the entire journey in the company of a man they called Geof Stein. Here, fortunately, he was

38

without suspicion. Geofry Stein, a man with a youthful face and a worried kind of crinkled forehead, talked a lot. He never said anything but his particular kind of volubility was reassuring, soothing and designed to extract information from the unwary.

'Stein, the Psych', a man with a prodigiously retentive memory had already extracted enough information from Ventnor to keep his department occupied for several months.

As a keen man, Stein was particularly interested in Ventnor's education. The man was highly intelligent but crippled by his limited vocabulary. Ventnor knew the word 'war' but not 'soldier'. He was familiar with 'spade' but he had never heard of a 'lathe'.

Stein was beginning to get a picture of how the Island was creating its stable society and, inwardly, he smiled bitterly. The society would be stable all right, safe, timid and, once freed, perish from sheer mediocrity.

The Islanders, in their desperate attempts to avoid a repetition of the recent destruction, were suppressing characteristics which were virtually survival reflexes.

The Padres intrigued him, too. He had ideas, but was too good a scientist to jump to conclusions.

The party passed through a clump of stunted trees and Ventnor found himself at the summit of a hill. Below, in the clear air, the countryside stretched undulatingly and greenly away to the horizon. Here and there, however, were black, burned-looking areas where nothing grew.

Stein touched his arm. "From here on stay very close to me. Try and put your feet where I put mine, this is a very dangerous pathway. On this pathway, or beside it, you may see things, very ugly living things. Most of them are harmless to man but they are still disturbing. Do not let them frighten you or cause you to disobey my instructions. If you do not do as I say and keep to the path, you will die. On the path it is safe, off the path it is not safe—do you understand?"

"Yes, I understand."

"Good, do not forget—follow me."

They began to descend, Peary leading the way. Seven flies—one of which was genuine—went with them.

The path wound slowly downwards through groups of

39

sickly looking trees which were so twined with ivy that among them it was almost dark. They slid down the walls of craters, the bottoms of which were still thigh-deep in wet gray ash. They crossed areas of burned soil entered another clump of trees.

Stein said, "Blood-toad ahead, it won't hurt you."

Ventnor looked at the thing Stein called a blood-toad and felt slightly sick. It was half as big as a man and looked like a transparent plastic bag half filled with scarlet liquid. There was no sign of eyes, limbs or eating orifices, but the thing stank revoltingly and the bag which was its body pulsated steadily.

Ventnor did not see it but when one of the 'flies' passed a moment later, the thing ejected a spurt of scarlet liquid knocking the tiny mechanism to the ground. The blood-toad, making squelching noises, undulated its body onto the top of it.

There were other things, bloated things which hung from branches and dripped. A thing like a hairless rat, its vital organs contained in little sacks on the exterior of its body —the little sacks were transparent.

Stein waited politely while Ventnor stood and retched. He was, however, not without feelings, he made some effort to draw the other's mind from his revulsion by pointing out the real dangers.

"See the bright sliver of metal in the trunk of that tree? Looks like a needle, doesn't it? It isn't a needle, it's a micro-cannon—a very small weapon—and, should you pass right in front of it, it will feel your body-heat. It is powerful enough to blow a hole as big as a man's clenched fist right through your body.

"That black tube on that stone over there is a chase-bomb. That, too, would kill you."

Stein did not go into the details of the chase-bomb. In his considered opinion it was the most diabolical weapon the human mind had ever conceived. Like most of the weapons of a dying culture, it was micro-constructed and justified its existence—if such a weapon could be justified —as a psychological deterrent.

The chase-bomb, once activated by body-heat, would rise with a whining sound and pursue its victim at slightly less than normal running speed. Sooner or later, of course, exhaustion would cause the condemned victim to lose the necessary speed and then the bomb would affix itself almost painlessly to his back.

There was no telling when it would blow, it might be six hours or six weeks. Any attempt to remove the bomb by any known means resulted in its immediate detonation so the victim became an outcast.

Understandably, an army, with twenty or thirty such carriers, among its units became completely demoralized. Even the desperate, if merciful, shooting of the carrier, only caused the bomb to fall off and lie in wait for the next victim.

Stein considered briefly the durability of these weapons. All of them were at least a hundred and twenty years old, yet all were functional. It was a curious paradox, and an unpleasant one, that the only mechanisms built to last had been killing machines.

They reached the foot of the hill at last and Peary breathed a sigh of relief and pushed the point of his spear into the soil. As he did so, a wristlet of what looked like human teeth, rattled slightly. The wristlet was appropriate to his appearance and in keeping with his cultural level but, in truth, all the teeth were micro-instruments.

Peary had checked carefully first to assure himself that the flies had been lost en route.

"Patrol G for George," he said.

"Receiving you George—nice work, but you're in trouble."

"Apart from the obvious, how come?"

"Our friends put down a ship between you and base. We think there's someone waiting. We can't use instruments to check in case detection instruments have been dropped too. I'm afraid you'll have to find him."

"Where and when?"

"The ship touched down about forty minutes ago, one to two kilometers dead ahead."

"Can we get past?"

"Not with a sporting chance, I'm afraid you'll have to take him. If you don't, he'll not only knock off the specimen, but, knowing the breed, all six of you as well."

41

"What a bearer of glad tidings you are—is the ship still around?"

"Not within detector range. You're safe enough from that angle."

"Condemn me with faint hope—right, over and out."

Peary pulled his spear out of the soil and climbed to the top of a nearby hillock.

Ventnor watched him completely bewildered. Already he was confused, frightened and completely at a loss. The sight of a man talking to a spear and the spear replying, was not only outside his experience but crippled his imagination.

On the hillock, Peary looked in his quiver and selected an arrow with red feathers. Then he held it up to his eye and appeared to look along it. In reality, however, he was looking through it. The missile was pierced and contained high-precision magnification equipment.

After a few moments he said, "Got him," to no one in particular. He manipulated a section of the arrow and within a shutter opened and closed. The cybernetic picture was transferred to the micro-memory banks and the reception acknowledged with a faint click.

Unhurriedly Peary unslung his cross-bow, fitted the arrow and raised the bow to his shoulder. . . .

V

THE KILLER SAT on a mound of earth at a spot once known as Hart Hill Crossroads. He was a thin man with crinkly dark hair, a pale cold face and curiously expressionless black eyes.

Trane did not regard himself as a killer, but as a soldier, a specialist with a precise task. He was a combat-technician undertaking alone a task which troops had once performed en mass.

The fact that he was compelled to justify his profession never struck him as a psychological weakness or caused him a moment of doubt. In truth he was completely self-contained and derived unashamed pleasure from his profession.

He was, he thought, probably the most intelligent 'soldier' ever permitted to bear weapons. Trane held degrees both in mathematics and bio-chemistry—an asset which made little difference to a psychology in which there were emotional deficiencies. To Trane, the words 'compassion', 'mercy' and 'affection', were meaningless symbols by which lesser men professed to be swayed.

For some forty minutes, with aid of special instruments, he had been watching the party of seven make their tortuous descent of Charing Hill. He could, of course, have picked them off as soon as they appeared, but that went completely against his nature. This was not only a killing, it was a hunt. The hunted should *know* of the hunter, otherwise half the satisfaction was lost. The fear, the desperate attempts to escape and the final despair, all were part of it.

Trane, however, was not made unwary by his eagerness. He was coldly and precisely efficient. Surrounding him, well within cross-bow range, were hollows, clumps of trees and other places where primitives might hide themselves. For all he knew half the tribe of the Maidstone boys may have surrounded him.

The idea rather intrigued him; they'd learn a lesson from which they would take many years to recover.

Trane wore a special suit, he carried a slender rifle with target-seeking micro-missile which exploded on contact. He had a deflector screen, warning devices and, in the event of mass assault, a wide-beam disrupter which was powerful enough to wipe out an old-time army division. In this respect Trane was right—he was a one-man army.

With detached curiosity he watched one of the party climb on a hillock and unsling his cross-bow. What the devil was the fellow playing at? Oh, probably some edible game; they couldn't possibly know he was here. In any case, no cross-bow ever devised could reach that far.

Trane was right—the crossbow couldn't, but the special arrow *could*. When his instruments picked it up and gave warning he thought it must have been fired by another primitive concealed close at hand.

He was not worried. He snapped on the deflector screen and made adjustments to his special contact lenses which slowed the light waves—the arrow became visible to him.

43

He turned to meet it, the deflector screen an invisible shield in front of him.

Strangely, less than twenty meters away, the arrow veered suddenly and alarmingly. He turned to meet it, keeping the screen between himself and the missile.

The arrow continued to turn, however, described a circle, and increased speed. Despite the contact lenses he lost sight of it.

He had no means of seeing—nor would he have believed —the micro-thrust units which were driving the arrow even faster.

He could hear the thin high whistle as it circled him and reached desperately for the disrupter. Maybe he could—

The sound changed abruptly, became a shriek which ended in a curiously muffled impact.

Trane staggered as if struck by a clenched fist, then he coughed wheezingly. Jerkily, he put both hands to his chest and, still coughing, fell to his knees. Blood ran from the corner of his mouth then, with both hands clasping the point of the arrow which protruded from his chest, he pitched forward on his face and lay still. Against the black material of his uniform the red feathers of the arrow were just visible. The missile had struck him just between the shoulder blades and passed completely through his body.

The party arrived a bare fifteen minutes later and Ventnor watched nonplussed as they went swiftly to work. The arrow with red feathers was skillfully withdrawn and an ordinary wooden one with green feathers inserted in its place.

Puttick, producing a variety of micro-tools from various parts of his person, went to work on one of Trane's instruments. When, in due course, it was examined, the investigators would find an apparently genuine defect. At the inquest, therefore, no one would worry particularly except, perhaps, some unfortunate technician who would be blamed for negligence. Trane had died, been shot by a primitive, because one of his instruments had failed him.

Once finished, the party moved off at a steady trot, anxious to put as much distance as possible between themselves and the body before the ship came back.

They arrived finally at a circle of huts which Stein for some mysterious reason referred to as Base 4.

Ventnor noticed immediately that although the huts were crudely built and varied in size, their arrangements was orderly. It was clear also that strict standards of cleanliness were enforced. The standards of sanitation equalled if not surpassed those of Del. Here was no, ever-present stench such as he had noticed in Hubel's Kingdom.

The party broke up and Stein led him to one of the larger huts. "You must be very tired and hungry. Food will be brought to you soon."

In a few moments a bearded man arrived with a tray of food on clean plastic utensils.

Stein said: "Eat!"

Ventnor ate ravenously but before he had finished, his stomach seemed to become heavy and his vision blurred. Stein's face seemed to expand and rush at him. "Sleep," it said. "Go to sleep now."

Ventnor was dimly aware that the world was slipping away, that he was falling sideways but knew that someone caught him before he fell.

When he awoke, he was lying on a rough but comfortable mattress in a smaller hut. He felt rested and remarkably clear-headed.

Stein sat beside him, cross-legged on a rough mat.

"Soldier," he said. "What do you understand by the word 'soldier'?"

Ventnor blinked at him. "Eh? I don't see—"

"Never mind what you don't see. Answer the question, please."

"Well—er—well, a soldier is a man engaged in military service." He sat suddenly bolt upright. "How do I know that? Yesterday I had only a vague picture of a man fighting."

Stein smiled. "Relax, Ventnor, I'll explain it in normal language. If there are words you fail to understand, tell me, but you should get the outline. The food you ate yesterday was drugged and, while you were unconscious, we not only took out all the information we could get but went to some pains to increase your vocabulary at the same time. We call it subliminal education. There are limits to it, but it was

45

ideal for that job. I must add here that anything else you want to learn will have to be done the hard way, by books and competent instructors.

Ventnor asked him the question which had been troubling him ever since he had been traded for a pair of binoculars and a razor. "Why have you gone to all this trouble, what's so special about me?"

Stein sighed and gave a brief outline of Island policy. "So you see you were important to us biologically. From you we have learned a great deal of the Island's methods and ultimate aims. We are very unhappy about it, but that's incidental."

He sighed again and smiled ruefully. "As for yourself, if it's any consolation, you're an inventive genius plus."

Ventnor paled. "A sort of super gadgeteer?"

"You can call it that, but don't let it worry you. Here we encourage it. As a matter of passing interest, Megellon had a bug about gadgeteers and he omitted stress-psychology. Starvation, disease and imminent death will turn any man into a gadgeteer if he thinks gadgeteering will spell survival. The world went mad trying to create things to stave off disaster."

Ventnor shook his head. "It's all a little hard to grasp at once and, on top of that, I feel strangely clear-headed. I *understand* things. It's like a new life, a new world. I know what cities are, guns, cars, surgeries, highways and castles."

He paused frowning. "It must have been a terrible war. All the cities wiped out, the bombs destroying millions—"

Stein looked at him strangely. "Yes, we took that from your mind too. They told you there was a gigantic war which almost completely destroyed humanity—this is where I have to do a little education myself: *It isn't true!*"

"Not true?" Ventnor looked at him blankly. "But the evidence is there. You pointed out the weapons to me yourself. I mean, the scars are still there, the weapons, repeater explosions, even the mu—mu—"

"Mutated is the word."

"Yes: the mutated animals."

Stein smiled sadly. "There was still no war, old chap. Oh, yes, there were some bitter and bloody skirmishes but they took place between armies and splinter groups number-

46

ing less than five thousand men. At no time was there the destruction or the clashing of enormous armies such as took place in World War One or Two. It is true attempts were made to take the Island, but these were the only occasions which could be described as full scale battles. Someone wrote a poem once: *"This is the way the world ends, not with a bang but a whimper."* That quotation is very true; the past perished in despair, weakly, and not in the furious upsurge of countless nuclear devices."

He rose. "I am not going to give you a history lesson. If you listen, observe and study the subject with an open mind, you'll reach the true answer yourself."

"What happens now?"

"For your own safety it would be advisable to remain with us. If you do, you must obey our laws and follow the mode of life laid down for other males of the community. You will be taught to use a cross-bow and you will be given commando training. We are a military community and, therefore, unless you have special talents—which you haven't— you must become a soldier. However, you will be given free time for study and education. Furthermore, every possible consideration and help will be given to any creative effort on your part."

Ventnor said: "Thank you." Then: "Won't they still be looking for me?"

Stein smiled. "Yes, but not for long. In due course, they'll find your body in a shallow grave about two kilometers from Hart Hill Crossroads. You see, their assassin got you before we got him."

Ventnor stared at him. "How?"

Stein shrugged. "People die, we use the body. Fortunately, our Island friends often blind themselves with their own science. They identify individuals by what they call the 'personality aura'. We altered the 'aura' to correspond with yours. In the clothing you will be given in a short time will be one or two mechanisms which will change the pattern of your present aura to something different."

Ventnor stood up. "Thank you again." He frowned at the other thoughtfully. "Tell me, am I being too clever with my new found knowledge? The most advanced mechanism

47

I have seen is a cross-bow—where are you finding all the rest."

Stein shook his head. "Can't tell you that yet but congratulations on your astuteness. In the meantime, you are a primitive, act like one. It is part of your duty."

Later, Ventnor was given fresh clothing and his body was stained to make it look filthy and he was conducted to a long hut with other recruits.

The same afternoon they were put through a course of physical training which left their muscles aching.

A month passed. Ventnor became leaner, harder and skilled in mayhem. He was taught in-fighting with a cutting spear and the skills of the cross-bow.

The cross-bow fascinated him—it was so simple yet so effective. On the other hand, reloading—

He asked permission to assemble and reassemble the device and sat pondering over the parts for a long time.

"Who makes these things?"

Gannon, another trainee with whom he had become friendly, pointed to a hut on the far side of the village. "See Walsh? I understand he's responsible for the general servicing."

Walsh, a grizzled elderly man with a limp moustache, listened to what Ventnor had to say and what he wanted, with boredom but his deep-set intelligent eyes were alert and interested.

"Have you any rough sketches I could work on?"

"Oh, yes! I've been attending evening classes, you know."

When Ventnor had gone, he pressed a section of what looked like the roof support of the hut and said: "Get me section three. Hello, that you Stein? Walsh here. I think your hunch has paid off. Our village lad has just dropped in with specifications for a new type cross-bow."

"To do what?"

"I don't know. He just placed an order for the parts. As for the rest, he's playing it close to his chest."

"Seems those evening classes I started were worthwhile."

"No doubt about it now, you owe a vote of thanks to all the recruits who went along to make it look genuine."

"More than a vote of thanks; that kindergarten stuff

must have bored them to tears. Most of them hold degrees in the advanced sciences."

"I know. I feel appropriately and sincerely grateful. I intend to arrange rewards for all of them as soon as they've finished the physical course."

Walsh sent for Ventnor a week later.

"I've got your parts—hope they suit."

"Thank you." The other picked them up and walked towards the door.

"You're not going to try them?"

"Yes, but not here. They might flop."

Walsh looked at him with sad humor. "Boy, you have all the makings of a true scientist—double test and secrecy, it's a natural reaction."

Ventnor, however, was back in an hour, his eyes excited. "It works, come and see!"

Just beyond the village he gave a demonstration and Walsh's eyes widened.

Under his breath he said: "Good God," in a shocked voice.

He pushed a caller into the soil and asked for connections to three departments.

"I suggest that all you gentlemen come up and see this. Our boy is not only a genius, he's a wizard and he's wasting his time up here."

All the observers arrived within half an hour and Ventnor demonstrated again.

The observers looked slightly shocked and Prone, director of Department 4, waddled over to look.

"Show me how it works, boy."

"Well, sir, the bow is first cocked by pulling this lever at the side. I then pull the trigger discharging the arrow. A system of opposing springs pushes the second arrow into place and, at the same time, recocks the weapon like this. Each—er—magazine holds eight arrows."

Prone scowled at him. "Tried out the rate of fire?"

"Not precisely, sir, but roughly forty-eight a minute which triples the rate over the normal bow."

"I see—thank you for the demonstration." Prone waddled back to the main party and scowled at Stein. "Well, now I've seen everything. I've seen some ingenious weapons in my time, I could name a dozen without thinking, but all of them were products of industrial cultures. This beats the lot. My God, outwardly this is a primitive culture, still is from Ventnor's viewpoint, yet with a piece of paper and a ruler he comes up with that thing. Gentlemen, do you know what he's built? I'll tell you—an *automatic cross-bow.*"

He paused and mopped his bald head. "Four springs, a lever, two clips and a box! One man puts them together and they become an automatic weapon."

He turned to Stein and pushed a pink finger into his stomach. "I want that boy, I want him in the labs. I want him trained, educated, aptitude-tested, guided and then let loose in the best facilities we possess."

Stein pushed the finger gently to one side. "It would take five years to do the job properly."

"Take ten if necessary—has he finished his physical?"

"Another two months."

"He'll have to finish it in his spare time as a recreation. I want him to start now, that's a priority order and I'll get it endorsed by the Council personally."

Ten minutes later Stein went over and tapped Ventnor on the shoulder. "You've made an impression—come with me."

He led the way into one of the huts, pressed a section of one of the roof supports and a section of rough-looking floor slid to one side.

"Down those steps."

Ventnor obeyed and found himself in a new and frightening world. They descended to a wide tunnel, a tunnel which was lit but possessed no lights—the wall of the tunnel itself gave out a bright radiance.

Here and there the tunnel was broken by doorways and Ventnor caught glimpses of shining machinery, banks of flickering lights and purposeful people clearly at work.

"Wasn't that Peary—that man in the white coat?"

"Yes—yes it was. We do three months in research and two months in the field. It is not only the rule here that keeps us fit and active. All that stuff above, you see, is a front, a disguise, an act to hide our real activities from the Island. If they knew, they would wipe us out and, as we are not yet strong enough for a showdown, we have to hide."

"I don't quite understand why."

"I don't suppose you do." Stein sighed. "I suppose I must fill you in on history otherwise it will affect your future education. I'll give it to you a bit at a time so you get a clear picture."

He led the way down a narrow side tunnel and continued the conversation over his shoulder.

"I'll give you the basic picture first and then I'll give you a session on the Recreator—I'll explain that when we use it."

They came to a room dominated by a huge machine on a raised platform.

"This is our local museum." Stein informed him.

Ventnor was still staring at the machine. He presumed it was some sort of vehicle, but it suggested both beauty and engineering perfection.

"What is it?"

Stein laughed softly. "Call it a symbol of courage. A vehicle built for endurance in the age of intransience. When the world was embracing short-life construction the people who built this refused to conform. They preferred their own integrity to easy profits. They perished but the symbol of their courage remains. As you can see, it's a vehicle—it was known as a Rolls Royce."

He sighed: "I understand Germany displays a Volkswagen, America a scalpel—a tribute to a certain manufacturer of surgical instruments who also refused to conform."

He sighed and led the way into another room. "Stand by, we are about to visit the age of intransience—"

VI

IN THE SECOND room were numerous articles on shelves in plastic containers.

Stein pointed. "Read the inscription on that—aloud, please."

"The Winsom Throw-Away Shirt."

"Fine, there is an article from the age of intranscience. A

51

shirt you wore once and threw away. If you wore it more than eight hours it fell to pieces on your body."

He paused and squatted uncomfortably on the edge of one of the shelves. "I'd better explain that the entire world had adopted the metric system although most of them retained their original symbols. America had always called their chief unit a dollar. We adopted the same system but still called our chief unit a pound—one hundred shillings to the pound. It is important to bear this in mind because these shirts were six a shilling.

"To be brief, the demand for manufactured goods was constantly increasing but, with the increase, the cost of producing goods rose also. Thus prices were constantly rising and people could not afford to buy. To avoid stagnation, wages had to be increased to meet the rising cost of living which, in turn, raised the cost of goods again—following me? Good. Obviously this continuous spiral would end in economic chaos but fortunately, or unfortunately, an industrial research group came up with 'short-life'. That is to say, substances such as plastics and metals which were cheap to manufacture and could be arranged to last only a short time.

"The trend had begun decades before with vehicles constructed to last only three years. Now, with the new cheap substances, the trend spread to almost every manufactured article. The politicians must have been delighted because the cost of living arrowed downwards and production rose to incredible heights. History shows, however, that this was a mistake."

Stein sighed and shook his head. "Sorry to bore you with dry facts, but let me give you a brief picture at the height of this economic 'boost' for that is all it was. You could, as I have said, buy six throw-away shirts for a shilling. An automobile, designed to last exactly three months, for twenty pounds. There were 'five-year-houses', 'ten-year-tenements' and 'six-week-washing-machines'. Even canned food was sold in short-life containers designed to last only a few weeks so that the purchasers would eat quickly and buy again.

"Needless to say, manufacturers and industrialists were reaping fantastic profits while the masses enjoyed unheard of luxury. In an effort to make more profit, the industrialists centralized and, in the end, the world's entire production was pouring from six great centers only.

"Centralization proved to be the primary mistake. In Europe, unexpected floods put one out of commission and, by a singular stroke of ill-fortune, a landslide cut the power supply of another.

"At the same time, in the United States, an airliner crashed out of control on a third wrecking the automatic control unit.

"The remaining three were compelled to supply not only the demands of the entire world but, at the same time, supply and dispatch vital spares and replacements for those out of commission. The auto-brains of two of these centers already over-loaded and over-taxed and, for that matter, over-programmed beyond their capacity, burned out under the strain. That was the beginning of the end. Efforts were made to get the centers moving again but as soon as one was repaired, another broke down casting an additional strain upon the rest. Since the products of one were dependent upon the products of another, the situation became hopeless. The food center was producing food but had reveived no bags or cans in which to pack it. In any case the transport center had not yet resumed production and, owing to short-life materials, existing methods of conveyance were failing every day."

Stein rose. "Have you followed me?"

"Yes, I think so."

"I hope you have, because I am now going to give you a session in the Recreator—this way."

The final room was small and, in the center of it, was a peculiar-looking high backed chair.

Stein waved to it. "Sit down, you are about to visit the past." He smiled as he attached sucker-terminals to Ventnor's wrists, his forehead and the back of his neck. "Do not be alarmed, you will not lose your identity. You will merely observe a period of history through another's eyes and another's faculties. You will become, for a brief period, a character we call Mr. Smith.

"This particular Mr. Smith, never truly existed. He is a composite character we put together for educational purposes. His experiences are composed of on-the-spot news

53

shots, mock-ups and a large number of emotional tapes recovered from the period, doctored in the continuity department and put together to create a precise character."

"Comfortable?" He patted Ventnor's shoulder but did not wait for an answer. "Fine, now relax, give yourself to the impressions which will flood your mind."

There was a faint click but Stein did not stop talking: "For your personal information, you are about to become a gadgeteer, the sort of gadgeteer that Megellon got a bug about. You will experiment with chemistry but you are not a chemist. You will try—and make—weapons—but—you—not—"

Strangely Stein's voice seemed to become a low humming and Ventnor experienced a momentary giddiness. An impression of light and shadow seemed to dance before his eyes and then he was staring at a circle.

The circle thickened, grew spokes—there was a feeling of movement, of buildings rushing by and the humming sound persisted.

Good God, he was driving a car—no!—Mr. Smith was driving the car but he, Ventnor, was a passenger in Mr. Smith's mind. He knew what Smith felt, feared and had experienced. He shared his memories, knowledge, doubts, dreams and apprehensions. And, at this time, at this moment, a burden of fear crouched in the back of Smith's mind.

Thank God, they'd sent the children up north—there was more food up there. Better not think of food—of course, the government would solve the problem, no doubt about that. There was this *protage* thing for instance. It was a kind of cabbage according to the news reports and contained all the necessary vitamins of well balanced meal. The thing could be planted on Monday and grew so quickly it was ready to harvest the following week.

Then there was the tuber, didn't grow so quickly, but was still a full meal and could be stored for months. Oh yes, most certainly the government would solve it—wouldn't they?

A thought struck him and he leaned forward and touched a small button on the dash. A light appeared and, in front of it, the numerals 10.

54

Ten days! Only ten days! He thought he had two weeks at the very least. Smith/Ventnor felt a cold wave of apprehension. At the end of ten days the service life of his car would be finished and, once finished it would either stop dead or refuse to budge from the garage.

There was, of course, another one on order. It had been on order for several months, but with things as they were—

There was public transport but that, too, was nearing the end of its short-life existence. Every day there were fewer buses on the roads and every day the monorail cut its services. What would he do without transport, how would he get to work?

The houses he was passing began to decrease in size and, within a few minutes he was in a residential area. He felt an illusory suggestion of safety as he turned the car into his own drive and nosed into the garage.

Safety, security—God, for how long? The house had only another six month's life.

It had seemed such a good idea once, modern, progressive, even visionary. Live in a house three years, move to a new modern residence for three more years. You were always ahead, always keeping up, but living cheaply—one hundred and fifty pounds every three years.

The houses you had left simply collapsed in a cloud of dust and the local council came along with a sucker-machine and cleared it away. If there was any modernization or street widening to be done, the council simply took advantage of the vacant space.

Smith/Ventnor scowled as he climbed out of the car. Yes, it had seemed a good idea once, had been when a three-year-house could be erected in eight hours, now, looking back, it was insanity. The people had nothing durable to fall back on. Even the tools and instruments of construction were short-life.

He entered the house conscious of hunger pains in his stomach, pains which reminded him that his breakfast had consisted of a single biscuit. Well, he was going to make a hog of himself now. He had one tin of beans which he had been hoarding for days. Once opened, it wouldn't keep so he'd have to eat it all—thank God.

55

He almost ran to the food cupboard and slid open the door.

Smith/Ventnor stared into the cupboard for several minutes then he put his head in his hands and cried.

The short-life can had fallen into pieces and the spilled mess on the floor of the cupboard was already giving forth an unpleasant smell.

After a time he shut the cupboard slowly and began to pace up and down. God, he was starving and he'd used his ticket for the sustenance ration, maybe there was some grass somewhere.

He shook his head, he'd seen too many people heading for the public parks with auto-mowers.

Synthetic food! The hypno-tutor! The four words seemed to come together in his mind in a kind of mental explosion. He'd collected hypno-tapes with the same enthusiasm some people collected books. His den was crammed with them.

He almost ran to his room and began to thumb desperately through the list of titles. Yes, yes, he knew he had one. *"The simple chemistry of synthetic foodstuffs."*

He almost jammed the tape into the tutor, placed the helmet on his head and switched on. God, yes, he'd make his own food, there were plenty of chemicals around, not to mention his ten-year-old son's chemistry set and all those bottles of stuff he'd brought when he'd dabbled in home-plastic-do-it-yourself jobs.

It never occurred to Smith—although the facts were communicated mentally to Ventnor—that no manufacturer of synthetic foodstuffs would permit his entire knowledge to be given freely to the public. The basic chemical construction would be given, yes, but not the final processing.

Later, Smith removed the helmet and switched off the hypno-tutor. He'd got it, he had every damn chemical, every one, enough to make a thick and sustaining soup for five days.

He found a large saucepan and went to work. Let's see, now, a gallon of water brought to the temperature of—

Within an hour he had a saucepan full of colorless rather repellent substance which, however, gave off a considerable amount of steam.

56

Smith tasted it cautiously—not bad but a bit tasteless, could do with a little salt maybe. With a total disregard for his own basic chemistry, Smith added a considerable amount of sodium chloride to his concoction.

He was about to ladle his dangerous meal into a soup plate when the doorbell rang.

Smith/Ventnor swore under his breath and went to the door.

"What in the name of hell are you playing at?" The policeman who asked the question was not a harsh man but he, too was hungry and, with the ever present threat of riots, his nerves were over-strained.

"What—?" Smith stared at him blankly.

"Don't play it stupid with me." The policeman grasped him by the lapels of his coat and jerked him forward. "A lot of people smelt cooking, a lot of hungry people. There's a mob forming and it's turning ugly. I've had to draft in a whole squad to keep order. They're saying you're a hoarder, an industrialist and God-knows-what."

"I'm not hoarding food." Smith, with a slightly uneasy conscience, was a little shrill. "I'm just trying to make something to eat synthetically."

"We don't give two damns what you're doing." The policeman pushed him back angrily. "For God's sake use a *little* sense." He scowled. "You could poison your damn self, you know that? Anyway, watch it, I'll clear this mob—if I can. In the meantime, draw your curtains and close your ventilators." He turned and strode away.

Smith drew the curtains hastily and shut off the ventilators. Outside he could hear the policeman shouting, there were answering jeers, scuffling noises and, finally, silence.

Smith sat down and ate. The mess was not particularly good: it tasted vaguely of wood pulp and sour milk. Nonetheless it eased his hunger and he went up to bed.

He woke in the night with his head throbbing and a swirling kind of nausea, but the feeling passed.

When morning came he reheated the remains of the substance, ate and went to work.

Scowling, suspicious faces watched him from nearby windows and a group of men on a corner shook their fists but there was no direct violence. He realized, however, that later there might be. He ought to get something to protect himself. He had a hypno-tape on weapons at home, maybe he could make something.

He stopped at a hardware store and made a few purchases.

"Twelve days life only." The autoserve informed him. "Consequent reduction sixty-five per cent."

When Smith reached the center of the town he became aware of drastic and frightening changes. Stalled cars, their life run out, littered the streets. Squads of men were pushing them to the side of the road but he was compelled to weave between the remaining cars.

The biggest shock, however, were the gaps in the familiar street. The 'Safety And Life' assurance building was a huge heap of dust which had spilled itself half-way across the road. 'General Purveyors' had also gone; 'Speedsafe Motors Inc', a warehouse—

When he arrived at his place of work—a finance company—the entire staff was standing outside.

"All right, you can go home, the computers have packed in." The area manager mopped his head despairingly. "We can get neither pens, papers or ledgers, so you can't even carry on with the simple stuff. In any case, half the sectors have sent us no figures to work on."

He suddenly glowered and waved his arms. "It's no damn good looking at me like that. I can't help it—go home."

Smith drove back slowly. There seemed more cars in the road and another building had collapsed.

An ambulance stood waiting in the road while a squad of volunteers dug desperately in the dust.

He stopped by one of several watching policemen. "What happened?"

"Obvious, isn't it?" The man looked at him as if he hated him. "There were thirty people still in the building, they knew its life was up but they couldn't belive it. In any case they had nowhere to go."

He thrust his chin forward suddenly. "Unless you can contribute something helpful, get out of here."

"Can I help?"

"We have a hundred volunteers but only twenty shovels—get moving."

Smith drove on and finally reached his home. Once inside he ate some more of the synthetic food and switched on the hypno-tutor.

Now, about the weapon—didn't want anything deadly did he? Just a deterent, something to stop a mob.

He went through the tapes—ah—yes—*Foundations of Nerve-Weapons.*

Again, it never occurred to him that the authorities would not permit the basics of even restraint weapons to be broadcast to all and sundry. The instructions were there, but they were not restricted to adults but could be obtained by adolescents over the age of sixteen.

It was intimated to Ventor at this point that Smith was representative of forty per cent of the population. A percentage using hypno-instruction to make both weapons and food—Megellon's gadgeteers.

Smith discarded his helmet and studied his purchases. He had all the necessary materials for the plastic casing—a Langley-Forge reaction crystal but no Raynor-tube. Maybe a Holz-Deven tube from the tri-dimentional would do as well, the idea was almost the same wasn't it? In any case the mere sight of a weapon might be enough and it would give him confidence in the event of trouble. All he needed now was a battery cell; there were no .05s in the place but he had two .03s, only slightly over the required power. Might take a little longer for the bloke to regain consciousness, say twenty minutes instead of ten, but that didn't matter, did it?

It was intimated to Ventnor here that the hypno-tutor, together with its tapes, was one of the crazes of the age. Large numbers of firms pushed the device with the same glowing promises that correspondence firms of dubious character had once offered to the hopeful and uneducated.

Can you play a musical instrument? Hypno-tuition can turn you into a master in less than twenty minutes.

Become a skilled operative—journalist—actor—director—financier—any damn thing by hypno-tuition. Unfortunately the hypno-impressions only lasted three months and then one was compelled to take another impression. This, however, did not stop the craze. It was so easy and gave such a boost to the ego.

Smith made himself some more synthetic food. This time, to him, the odor was less savory and it required considerable effort to force the substance down his throat.

Just as he was finishing, the window behind which he was eating, bulged inwards and twanged back into place. The heavy stone was flung back dangerously at the man who had thrown it.

Suddenly cold, Smith saw that an angry mob was gathered outside the house. *Damn!* He had forgotten to draw the curtains again.

He picked up the home-made gun, went to the door and opened it a crack.

"Get away from here. I'm not doing you any harm."

They shouted: "Hoarder," and "Industrialist," at him and a big man with an unshaven face shook his fist.

"We've got starving kids, while you sit and eat regular meals."

"His wife ran away with a black-marketeer," shouted a woman shrilly. "He was too low even to feed her."

They shouted again, surged forward and the unshaven man kicked open the gate.

"What you want is a sharp, hard lesson."

Smith pushed the barrel of the weapon through the crack in the door. "You come another damn foot and I'll use this."

The man laughed. "What have you got, little man—a water pistol? Think you can scare me with that toy?"

He snatched suddenly at the weapon crushing the door on Smith's hand and pressing in the firing stud.

There was a sound and a curiously livid scarlet flash. The man staggered and was suddenly covered in a multitude of tiny blue and green sparks.

Literally frozen, Smith watched him totter away from the door, a set-piece in a firework display, a grotesque pearly king with blue and green pearls—*Oh God!*

The man seemed to fall suddenly when he was half-way down the path. When the body struck the ground, gray dust puffed from his clothes and a cloud of glittering sparks danced briefly above the body like a swarm of fireflies.

60

Smith was aware of the mob racing away in panic, of the sparks blinking out one by one and the somehow shapeless body sprawled on the path.

Numbly he shut the door, locked it, piled tables and chairs against and repeated the performance at the back. Then he sat down and made to put his head in his hands —hands? What was the matter with his hands, goose pimples? *Blue* goose pimples?

VII

HE STARED at the hands a long time and then put them behind his back. It didn't matter; there was a dead man in the middle of his path. A man he had killed with a 'safe' weapon. Oh God, what·had he made?

Smith became slowly aware of a strange inability to concentrate and remember. What was he worrying about? Oh, yes, the man, the dead man—would that be the same man Molly had run away with? No, that was Harris—the dead man wasn't Harris. God, he felt *sick*—so blasted *sick!*

When, six hours later, a mob rushed the house under cover of darkness, he was still sitting there.

He was still alive but he couldn't hear them and he couldn't see them.

The mob leaders looked at the distended body, the grotesquely swollen hands, the blue balloon-face and backed hastily away. Once they called his name hoarsely, then they turned and ran . . .

Ventnor shook himself, opened his eyes and looked at Stein. He made no comment but there was a kind of sickness in his eyes and his face was pale.

"I'm sorry." Stein was brusque. "Everyone has to go through it, everyone has to learn. All you experienced happened every day, some of them, as you have learned, stumbled upon the most dreadful weapons.

"As for the food, God knows what some of them concocted, but they left a terrible legacy behind them. The scavengers and micro-organisms which consumed their bodies under-went certain changes, in the course of generations, as a result. In consequence, we had changing life-forms and new and often virulent micro-organisms."

Stein paused then said, quickly. "No, don't move, we might as well get the rest over, there's more to come."

"More!"

"Afraid so, old chap. You are about to become an Engineer, a certain George Lansom. Lansom is—was—not a composite character. He was a living man, a skilled technician. Somewhere he had found a 1982 diary which, of course, was made of long-life materials. In this diary he carefully recorded his daily experiences and, so intense were his emotions and feelings, that we were able to get viso-emotional recordings from almost every page."

There was another click and Stein continued. "Lansom lived in the years of despair and fought in the last bitter battles before the final collapse. This was several—years—after—Smith—"

The voice seemed to fade, lose meaning, become liquid like the sigh and slap of water.

There was water, gray choppy water and a cool damp wind blew steadily in Ventnor's—no—Lansom's face. Yes, gray cold water, the sea, with darker gray clouds in watery masses in the dull evening sky.

Ahead of him, and on either side, were boats, hundreds and hundreds of boats. Ancient motor yachts—now laboriously propelled by oars—crude rafts supported by bulks of timber, things with sails, sweeps and foot-driven revolving paddles. There were even a few plastic paddle-boats— once of the sport of the holiday-maker—how many years ago was that?

All the boats were packed with men, most of them bearded, all of them emaciated and every one burdened with arms. In a few hours they would be hidden by darkness and, in that darkness, they would land unseen on the beaches. Then, by God, look out Indoes, look out you blasted industrialists and tycoons, the Engineers are going to stamp you into the ground. -

The part of Lansom which was Ventnor and seeing the scene the Lansom's eyes became suddenly aware of curious familiarity. Hadn't he been here before? Those high white cliffs, that spur of chalk, that mound and the flat coast which they had left in the early afternoon. *That was Del!*

Only it wasn't Del, not in Lansom's mind, it was a place called *Deal*. Gret was *St. Margarets Bay* and their destination was a place called *Dover*.

Ventnor recalled a pile of rubble on a high hill, the outlines of a huge city, gouge-cats, Berman and a chalky stream.

Then, strangely, the memories seemed to fade and Ventnor, succumbing to stronger emotions became, almost completely, George Lansom.

Lansom was not a nice man, not now, not after all that had happened. Had been once, years ago. There had been reasons then, standards, affection, warmth, security and of course, the—

To Ventnor something closed in Lansom's mind with the savagery of a rat trap, a kind of defensive rat trap, biting out a memory which hurt too much to think about. He had a glimpse of tiny hands and little laughing faces—*Daddy!* —Daddy!—

Then it was gone and in its place was hate. The bloody Indoes, they'd done it, hoarding the food, letting the world fall to pieces. But they'd pay, yes, they'd pay! That was why he was in this boat, loaded down with weapons with the damp sad wind blowing in his face.

Strangely, Lansom was not afraid. He was an experienced fighter with no illusions, but fear did not touch him. All he wanted was to get as many Indoes as possible.

In the fading light, Lansom rechecked his weapons. They were good weapons and he had made most of them himself. All of them were long-life stuff, made from the parts of an ancient Rolls Royce, a case of American surgical instruments and, of course, constructed with a set of Italian long-life precision instruments which had been given to him by his father. They'd been a showpiece once, kind of a relic, outmoded but interesting to visitors. They'd stood on a shelf in his room once under glass and Mary—Oh, Mary, darling—*Mary!*

In Lansom's mind the rat trap closed again, shutting out the memory.

63

Two hours later his boat grated on sand and he sprang out with the others and went crunching noisily up the beach. It was strange that no one had heard them because already the shore line was crowded with dark figures, many of whom had already scaled the crumbling sea wall.

As they crossed the coast road, a watery moon broke through the low clouds and Lansom was conscious of a curious sense of disappointment. In the faint light Dover was like any other town, the same mounds of dust, the same half-buried streets, the same dusty desolation.

He had half-expected buildings, lighted windows even, perhaps, the sounds of music. Here, however, was only the sigh of the sea wind and the dreary, dusty desolation.

Lansom stiffened almost unconsciously. This was a trick, a typical Indoe deceit. Somewhere they were waiting in readiness. The Indoes had always been cunning and treacherous but not clever, not really clever. The repeaters for instance—cunning but not clever. Oh yes, they'd stopped the overland attack all right, but there was a certain bestial stupidity in a weapon you couldn't stop yourself.

Lansom thought briefly about the repeaters. They could go on blowing for centuries, hour after hour, for centuries. No one could dismantle them for the projectors were protected by the force of the explosions they created. They would never run dry because they were solar-powered and drew their energy from normal light. They drew enough power in daylight to keep going all night so you were beaten all round.

There was nothing really startling about them technically. You took a G-type Markham projector and an L-type Markham projector and set them up about a kilometer apart. You then directed the beam of type G and the beam of type L to meet at a given spot or, what the experts called 'agitation point'.

The beams excited the molecules of the atmosphere, eventually causing an explosion. It was not quite a nuclear explosion, it was more an electronic explosion. The point was, however, it was unpredictable, sometimes it blew seven times in an hour and, at other times, seven times a day. Several hundred had tried to put the things out of

64

commission and several hundred had died. Close approach seemed to trigger it.

They continued to advance, ankle deep in dust, crouching, weapons ready, and tense for the surprise attack.

The sea was nearly five hundred meters behind them before light stabbed from a mound of rubble some hundred meters ahead.

Some distance to Lansom's left a curious scarlet bubble rose suddenly from the ground and he saw that a man was enveloped in it. The trapped man made convulsive movements with his limbs then pitched forward on his face. As he fell the scarlet bubble vanished as if pricked by a pin.

A hoarse voice shouted: "Take cover! Bubble cannon!" And then he heard the liquid monkey-chatter of a home-made Hersholt as a group of men on his right laid down answering fire.

The mound of rubble from which the bubble cannon had fired began to glitter, turned slowly to a shimering white and puffed upwards jet of sparks.

They advanced again but now resistance was stiffening. Light stabbed from numerous mounds and men began to fall.

Ahead there were warning shouts: "Micro-cannon! Mine field here!" And then, urgently: "Chase-bombs! Watch out —chase-bombs!"

Two cursing men suddenly drew level with Lansom and dropped flat behind a low mound of dust. Something bulky lay between them. He recognized the squat outlines of what was popularly known as a 'muck-spreader'. It was in actuality a composite, long-range micro-cannon with thirty barrels; the weapon fired explosive missiles no bigger than the point of a pin at the incredible rate of eighty missiles a second per barrel.

The two men sited the weapon carefully, then one lay flat and began to stab the firing keys with the speed and skill of an expert touch-typist.

The weapon only made a curious sighing sound but, far ahead, a tremendous area of ground boiled and spurted yellow flame. The ever-present dust swirled up with it in a cloud and began to roll outwards and towards them.

65

Lansom's ears hurt from the reverberating noise that rolled and echoed outwards from the fire.

Suddenly the noise stopped and the two men climbed to their feet. One of them grinned, white teeth showing briefly in the darkness. "That shook the bastards, eh? That taught them a lesson."

They picked up the heavy weapon between them and went on. Lansom followed; through the pall of dust the flash of weapons far ahead looked sullen and angry.

He came upon three men setting up a sonic mortar.

"Heard the news? We've got them on the run. They've pulled out of the inland defences but Kirby's lot cut them off at Buckland Bridge. Those who got clear are pulling back to the Castle."

"Be a hard place to take."

"Not with this." One of the men patted the mortar lovingly. "That place may be long-life and thick but once we get accurate readings on the structure of the stone a couple of missiles from this will kick it apart like a house of cards. The missiles are keyed to set up vibrations, see? Like a high note shatters a wine glass, clobbers a man's brain as well."

Lansom went on. A cold wind blowing in from the sea was clearing the haze of dust and making his thin body cold. A paleness in the sky warned of the coming dawn.

He was not happy about it, from the commanding heights of the castle the Indoes could cover the whole area and there was very little cover.

He had covered only a few more meters when he was brought to a halt by a number of shallow foxholes and several armed men.

"Front line, mate, we're assembling for attack—what's your mob?"

"I'm in Benson's lot."

"Benson? Oh, yes, you'll find his crowd on what used to be Pencester Road. Follow the foxholes that way."

Three minutes later Lansom was among the men he knew, most of whom were digging shallow foxholes with their hands. He followed suit then squatted in the hollow he had made and ate his last ration of food—a cube-shaped piece of dried *protage* which was, he thought, about the size of a lump of sugar. Inwardly he laughed harshly—what the hell was sugar? He tried to remember when he had last eaten a full meal. The time he and Squire had caught that wild cat or was it when they'd stewed a couple of rats and seagull? Couldn't remember properly; funny there were no seagulls around here. No, not so strange when you came to think about it. So much of the land poisoned by this and that, and they said the sea was still badly polluted near the coast. He'd noticed the stink as they came in, kind of a sickly chemical smell.

He realized it was almost light and looked upwards. Above them, surprisingly close, the castle stood remotely against the sky.

He studied it almost detachedly. It looked high, far away, grayly serene and somehow unreal. A ragged gray cloud drifted above seeming almost to touch the battlements.

He remembered when he had first seen it—twenty—thirty years ago? Been a showplace then, ancient monument, a genuine Norman Castle. He'd been in it, paid five shillings. When they'd got to the battlements he and Mary had lifted the kids up so that—*no!*

He forced the memory from his mind and studied the approach. Steep and bare, no cover at all, this was going to be worse than Charing.

It was then, that far away, a man put two fingers between his lips and emitted a piercing whistle.

The sound produced a curious electric tension. This was *it!*

There was another whistle and, behind them, a 'muck-spreader' opened up with a sighing sound.

The lower slopes of the hill vanished, became a sea of yellow flame, a cauldron of reverberating explosions and swirling smoke.

"Forward!"

With a numb kind of obedience Lansom found himself advancing with the rest. They walked into the black smoke left by the 'muck-spreader', stumbling over the still hot soil and lurching into craters.

Lansom was not frightened but he was tense and aware of increasing fatigue. How old was he—fifty-seven—sixty?

They came out of the smoke, crouching both from experience and the steepness of the slope. There was no real cover; the trees and hedges had been cut down long ago. Only the lines of pathways and the cuttings in the chalk which had once held public benches showed that this blackened hill had once known peace.

Slightly ahead of him a man grunted, put his hands to his stomach and fell sideways. For a second he clung with one hand to a projection in the ground, then the body went limp and rolled back down the hill into the still swirling smoke.

"Micro-cannon!"

They spread outward and away, flat on their bellies like snakes.

Lansom eased a search instrument from his belt.

"Between them two flat stones, keep your heads down!"

There was the thud of a compression pistol and then smoke and flame swirled about them as the micro-weapon together with its magazine, was blasted out of existence.

They rose to the crouching position again and went on. Then, behind them, a voice shouted: "Clearway—carriers! Stand clear—carriers!"

The line broke, scuttling from left to right, throwing themselves desperately flat.

Three men passed between them unhurriedly, blank-faced, crouching only from the steepness of the slope. All carried conventional weapons but they seemed to scorn cover. They went steadily ahead, silent, with a kind of blind unfaltering determination.

A man near Lansom raised his head slightly and his mouth twisted. "Get well up there, boys. We don't want you copping a packet half-way and rolling back on us."

Lansom was not shocked by the man's crudeness. In part he shared his feelings—the three men were doomed anyway. *Between the shoulder blades of each one was the black leech-blob of a chase-mine.*

Lansom thought, briefly, that they'd learned a lot since the Charing campaign. Then, those damn chase-bombs had demoralized them completely but the bitterness of defeat had taught them other methods. They called it the Kamikaze technique—a carrier, knowing he was doomed, simply stood up and walked into the enemy lines.

Lansom smiled bitterly, and that exquisite touch had carved up the enemy's morale more than their own. Their own lovely little weapon had bounced back right in their faces.

He watched the three figures draw away, become smaller until it seemed they were almost beneath the castle walls. Then remotely, there was an explosion, followed by two others. A cloud of black smoke rose in the air and was slowly carried away by the wind.

"Amen," said the man near Lansom without reverence or particular regret. "They've had it—come on."

The line rose and went forward again.

Far behind them the sonic mortar went into action. They did not hear the reports but they heard the missiles pass high above them with a curious liquid sound.

They froze, waiting, bearded, haggard faces turned upwards, watching.

There was no explosion, no flash, no smoke. Dust trickled briefly, then, slowly, with a kind of despairing weariness, a huge section of the wall crumpled and fell inwards. Seconds later, one of the turrets swayed uncertainly and crumpled in on itself.

Dust rose, drifting like smoke, spreading outwards, seeming to mix with the slow gray clouds which drifted just above.

The men did not cheer; they looked at one another tiredly and, as if in mutual agreement, trudged on.

Before they had reached their objective, many of them fell —limp, sprawled things without meaning or cause for regret. No one bothered to see if they were still alive, the badly wounded would die anyway, the rest would crawl away. There were no hospitals, no first aid and worst of all, no hope. Even the slightly wounded, unless they were very lucky, would soon join the other nameless dead. There were new micro-organisms in the poisoned soil against which there was no defense.

Lansom trudged on with the rest, conscious of an ever-growing fatigue and a curious sharp pain in his chest. It felt as if someong had been working on his heart with needle and thread and drawn the stitches tight.

Eventually they reached the remains of the castle, the

69

great stones piled one upon another in untidy heaps. Some of the vast high rooms were still precariously intact, but the ceilings sagged dangerously in places. Dead Indoes lay in heaps but Lansom found himself looking at them with horror. These were not the well fed, arrogant industrialists about which he had been told. These were tired, emaciated bearded men, many of them grizzled like himself. There were women, too. He moved to another room, sat down on a huge stone and, almost from habit, removed his diary from its long-life tin box. The stub of long-life pencil which he had found in Deal would not be any good much longer but would probably outlast him.

Today we took Dover from the sea. The landing was easy, but when we went inland—

His writing was interrupted by shouts and three struggling men stumbled into the room. One had the symbol of an officer painted on his back and the other two were striking him with their fists.

"You lied to us—where's the food? You said there was food here, you bastard."

The officer fell down and they began to kick him. "Where is the *food?*"

Lansom shared their resentment but it was directed more against himself. He'd been 'taken'. There had never been any Indoes, at least not the fat, well-fed Indoes about which they had been told. This was a rabble army of half-starved scarecrows like himself.

Almost automatically he went on writing: *Payne was killed in the first few minutes—*

It was getting dark early, wasn't it? Surely the air wasn't thin up here—why was—he panting? His chest hurt—hurt—Mary—Mary—the kids—where—

VIII

When Ventnor opened his eyes, Stein was a little shocked to see tears in them.

"You must be very sensitive."

"Really?" Ventnor sounded a little choked. "I don't know, maybe I read deeper—is it wrong to react?"

70

"If you mean do I disapprove—the answer is no. Most definitely no! Although as a psych I shouldn't, I despise the indifferent. I've had young girls through this thing and some of them haven't batted an eyelid." He sighed. "Candidly, I distrust lack of feeling, so you have gone up in my estimation, although, I must add here, it will make you very vulnerable."

He paused and began to remove the terminals. "Lansom was fifty-eight when he died, heart attack as you probably guessed."

Ventnor looked up at him. "And all he fought for, all he cared for was his wife and children. He fought, killed the Indoes, hated, because it eased the aching sense of loss inside him."

Stein nodded. "Very touching. Not many get to the actual motivation of the man." He changed the subject. "Not a pretty story, those final days."

"And now we rebuild?"

"Where it is possible without the Island finding out—rebuild and, more important, profit by past mistakes."

He laughed briefly and bitterly. "Some of us have a 'thing' about the Island. They're so God-awful blind and so smug with it. They conduct this grandiose experiment on the commandments of a deceased paranoic. Megellon, as I have told you, had a bug about Gadgeteers. He also had a bug about religion—hence the Padres. Here is the perfect example of a man who thought he was God trying to create a race of sheep in his own image. His kind of sheep, once the work is complete, won't survive two generations alone. Meanwhile, the world itself is sliding to pieces. Soil erosion has already turned Africa into one huge Sahara and dust bowls are spreading in the United States, Australia and many parts of Europe.

"While the Island conducts itself like an Olympus creating their alleged stable society, vital work goes unnoticed. The world needs not these pathetic culture trays, but vast engineering projects, the rebuilding of cities and the foundation of a new society educated to the mistakes of the past."

Stein paused and smiled grimly. "You are probably unaware that the 'primitives' outside the culture trays, are permitted to continue their existence only for 'comparison purposes.' What they do not know is that, but for our forebears, there would be no primitives.

"People like Hubel, and thousands of such tribes all over the world, owe their existence to those who stayed behind in survival cells. This base for example, began with forty men and women working in an artificial cavern under a hill near Lenham.

"With strictly limited equipment, awful conditions and working like dogs, they virtually saved this area. The same tales of heroism can be applied to every resistance cell in the world. In England, the United States of America, Europe, in fact almost every part of the world, these tiny groups of dedicated experts worked until they dropped, staggered to their feet and worked until they dropped again.

"They planted protage and tuber in every fertile patch of soil. They cleansed poisoned soil and purified the polluted rivers and streams. Working against time in impossible conditions they studied the new diseases and came up with new antibiotics. Every band of vagrants who wandered into the area was knocked out with sleep gas and innoculated to a man. Later, as they grew in experience and knowledge, they were able to include immunization factors into the cell growth of protage and tuber so that the survivors built up resistance from their normal diet. This, however, took several years, in fact nearly a generation to develop."

Stein paused and sighed. "Suppose I've said enough for one day. Next thing is to get you settled in, fix aptitude tests and start the education program. You, too, my friend, are going to work like a dog—"

Ventnor soon discovered that these were not idle words. A system of what was known as 'intensive education' had been worked out some years before and he was given the full treatment. It had nothing to do with hypno-tuition or subliminal education techniques but it achieved results. So skillful were his instructors and so unique were the methods employed, that a complete school term—by the old methods —was packed into a single week.

At the end of two months, therefore, he had graduated. He was helped by his lively intelligence and his overwhelming desire to learn. He was unaware at the time, however, that aptitude tests had been skillfully included in the program and that his instructors were carefully paving his way.

So busy was he both with the educational program and the rigorous physical training that he barely had time to study this base. He knew there were extensive laboratories and limited recreation facilities but beyond that he knew very little. If he was not learning, he was on field work, or going through the final stages of advanced mayhem. At this stage he was beginning to find himself as an individual and, although enjoying the training from a competitive viewpoint, deplored the uses to which his knowledge might have to be put. He had no active desire to kill a man and recoiled at the thought of doing so.

He soon learned by chance conversation that there were forty-five other bases like his own in the country and they were not unique. In the United States there were two hundred and eight, in Europe, one hundred and eighty, in Canada and Australia one hundred and fifty and so on. All had the same record of devotion, self-sacrifice and the spirit of complete dedication as those in his own country.

What did surprise him, however, and when he learned how, no little inward amusement, was the fact that all the bases worked in the closest and friendliest co-operation. This was due to the fact that the old tele-cables had been overlooked or forgotten by the Island. As these cables were long-life, they had survived the period of intranscience and had required only power and minor repair to get them going again.

As the majority of the cables passed on the bed of the ocean directly beneath the Island there was a certain ironic humor in sending a message say, to Manhattan Base 3, right under the enemy's stronghold.

In his second educational year, he struck up an acquaintance with Judith.

Judith was blonde, sensual and calculating. She collected men and physical experience with the same intensity of purpose that greedy people reserve for money. Ventnor's background also appealed to her and, all too clearly, he was brilliant and on his way up.

She lacked the self-honesty to acknowledge that she

73

would soon weary of all these attractions. He was new, he was there and Judith lived only for the present.

There was no real subtlety about her and, although she played it straight, she did so with considerable skill. She had a striking full-breasted figure and she virtually threw it at him.

Ventnor, over-sexed and inexperienced, went down before the first assault.

Prone and Stein watched the association begin with considerable misgiving.

"It would be her." Prone was scowling. "She's a brilliant biologist but as a personality she's worthless."

"He'll be hurt." Stein was thoughtful. "Badly hurt, but in the long run she'll smother him. He's extremely sensitive and he'll soon become aware of her lack of any real feelings."

"Blast her feelings," said Prone, sourly. "What about *his* work?"

Stein's prediction, however, proved to be correct. Ventnor soon discovered that he wanted something deeper than a beautiful responsive body. Somehow behind the hungry lips there was a coldness and absence of real feeling which he sensed but could not put into words.

To Prone's delight and Stein's relief he began to devote more time to study and field work.

Judith for her part, began to feel his lack of response. It was a new experience for her. She was used to men she could throw aside when she wearied of them. It was her first experience of the reverse side of the coin and she became possessive and bitter.

"You may be Prone's white-haired genius but for God's sake try and be a human being—have you taken vows or something?"

When he did not answer she tried the same line from other angles. "I suppose, now you've used me for your pleasure, I am to be thrown aside. You used to ask me to marry you."

"And you always refused." He reminded her sharply. "You said and I quote: 'Marriage is the refuge of the emotionally insecure'."

74

She called him an obscene word, then: "I supposed all this is due to that bitch, Gina."

"Gina!"

"Oh, don't play it innocent. You stop at her desk every time you come in from patrol."

"I have to. She's the base allocator. Any specimens—"

"I know what she does, thank you. She takes soil samples of anything you bring in and sends them to the appropriate departments for analysis. She's a sorter, a menial—no degrees, no scientific qualifications whatever."

She paused and came closer to him. "You haven't a thing in common, yet you spend about half an hour chatting —people notice, you know."

"You mean, you've noticed."

"All right, I've noticed. What is there between you two?"

He rose. "Nothing so far as I am aware, but I must congratulate you on some excellent match-making. You're not only putting ideas in my head but you're throwing me at her as well."

"I'm sure she'll do an excellent job of catching you."

He sighed. "Judith, this is the fifth row in two weeks. All of them, like this one, were about nothing. Let's forget it, shall we?"

"No, we won't forget it. Do you think I don't realize you're cooling off? You think you can use me and throw me aside like some damn primitive woman from the villages. Who do you think you are?"

He turned his back on her. "I have a patrol to do. While I am away try and think this over calmly."

"Why don't you say 'get lost' and have done with it?" She made for the door but turned as she opened it. "Right, this is the finish, but don't think I've finished with you. Never think that!" The door crashed shut behind her.

An hour later Ventnor left the collection of huts which concealed the base with a feeling of relief. Not only had he discovered that he hated scenes but that this final one had somehow severed everything.

For a long time he had been conscious of Judith's lack of genuine feeling and her coldness. It was a coldness which had nothing to do with her concupiscence—after all this had begun because she had invaded his sleeping quar-

75

ters at night. No, the truth was, although she derived intense satisfaction from the physical association, she felt nothing inwardly. Not that he himself was blameless. At first he had been completely swept away by desire for her and, in that desire, had been something like love. But she had cut that down before it could develop: "Don't get maudlin, darling. I find it emotional and rather repugnant."

Ventnor pushed the subject from his mind. It was a good thing it was over and done with.

He strode on and, four hours later, was near his objective. The territory was unfamiliar but he was now an experienced field worker and finding it had presented no real problems. The only snag—and one which did not trouble him particularly—was the fact that it bordered on dangerous territory.

Slowly, because it was a formidable task and because there were more urgent and immediate problems, the various bases were pushing their way back into the great cities.

It was no easy task; cities like London, New York, Berlin, or Paris had been the stages not only for intense fighting but hot-beds of Gadgeteers.

Although these things were past, the weapons they had used remained. The earth was poisoned, the water polluted and every square meter was dangerous in one way or another. On the surface, the gouge cats, bands of hairless dogs and other things roamed unchallenged. No-one knew what dwelt in the ancient subways and the deep tube systems.

Ventnor's mission, however, was simple enough: An area of land on the outskirts of London had recently been sprayed with purifying chemicals. It was his business to check the effects, make tests, take soil samples and drop cleansing agents into any water source in the immediate area.

He reached his destination and, topping a slight rise, came to an abrupt halt. Far away, across what was literally a desert of dust, and catching the early afternoon sun was a dome. He knew what it was but he had never seen it before.

There, still far on the horizon, as remote as the pyramids, but still conveying a solemn beauty was the dome of St. Paul's Cathedral.

Ventnor, absently sucking a slight scratch on his thumb

which he had acquired somewhere on the journey, stood staring at it a long time. Mentally he raised his hat to the men who had gone out of their way, probably at considerable risk, to preserve these long-life buildings. Buildings 'haunted' by one or two solar powered long-life projectors and some timed sound-tapes.

He sighed and turned his attention to the business at hand.

After only a few minutes work he frowned and sucked his thumb again which was throbbing slightly. It was badly swollen.

Ventnor had been given precise orders in the event of wounds and he dusted it hastily.

The throbbing stopped but ten minutes later began again.

Ventnor did not waste time wondering if the matter was trivial or not; orders were strict on the subject. He pushed his spear into the soil and called base. The method of communication using the earth's natural magnetism was limited in range but was indetectable to normal radio devices.

"Receiving you, Robert, go ahead."

"Section 7, please."

"Check—connection, section 7."

"Hello, section 7. This is patrol, R for Robert. I have a scratch on my right thumb. I have dusted it but relief was only temporary. My thumb is now nearly double the normal size and turning blue—instructions, please."

There was a slight pause, then: "Right, Robert, drop what you're doing and make for base fast."

"There's nothing in my first aid kit—?"

"Nothing. Make for base but call in every ten minutes, *every* ten minutes—clear?"

"Understood—over and out."

Ventnor packed his equipment hastily and began to stride back, aware of a cold dampness at his temples. Section 7, medical branch, had not actually said anything alarming but the implications were there. This was no minor septic infection, this was something they *knew* about.

In section 7, Medical Director Culbertson, pressed the

emergency switch. "All departments, full alert—get me Director Graham, please."

Graham's brown harsh face swam suddenly into the screen. "Yes, Culbertson?"

"Your endorsement on a Class-2 emergency, please. We have a patrol in trouble—suspected case of Hartman's disease."

Graham's mouth seemed to thin. "That's Blue-burst, isn't it?"

"Yes, I'm afraid it is."

"Class-2 emergency endorsed. I'll check patrols. Someone will have to go out and bring him in before—"

"A routine patrol won't do, sir. We have to send special anti-toxins and Hartman serums from this section right now."

"Check." Graham vanished from the screen but his face reappeared in less than a minute. "Culbertson, we're in a spot. Our nearest patrol is twenty kilometers from base and thirty from your case."

"What have we got here?"

"Basic defense only." Then savagely: "I'm sorry, but you know the rules. I can't endanger the entire base for one man. I know it's harsh but to make it clearer—suppose we suddenly run up against five other cases?"

"You've made your point, Director." Culbertson, usually mild mannered, was suddenly violently aggressive. "But, surely to God, there's *someone*? Damn you, man, what about clerks, technicians—"

"Don't try and tell me my job, Mr. Culbertson. I've checked! Every man, not actively essential, is on light duty and you know what that means. It means that every one of them has some minor complaint. *You* know, far better than I, what will happen if you approach a case of Blue-burst with even a head cold—it will mean death."

Culbertson said: "Oh, God!" Then: "Look, will you do one last favor—broadcast a call for volunteers? There may be someone we have overlooked. After all, women have training—they have to in case we have to pull out of base in an emergency."

"You're snatching at straws, Culbertson." He scowled. "There could be a chance, however, hold on—"

Less than eight seconds later, the speakers were booming:

78

"Attention all hands. This is Graham speaking. A Class-2 emergency is in operation and volunteers, excluding B1 and C4 sections, are urgently required for a dangerous mission. One of our patrols, R for Robert, has contracted Blue-burst and anti-toxins must be rushed to him immediately. Will any member of this base, who may have been missed in our previous checks, report to my office immediately, repeat, *immediately—time is vital.*"

Twenty minutes later Judith entered the office. "I heard there was an emergency call—I'm sorry, I was asleep."

Graham did not look up from his desk. "Get lost, Miss Lane."

She flushed. "I don't understand, I came as soon as—"

"You came after a twenty minute delay which you well knew could prove fatal."

"That's not fair, I—"

Graham looked up at last and his eyes were cold. "Miss Lane, I run this base. You don't see much of me in normal routine, but I know what goes on, it's my job. I put it to you, you let your private entanglements, your passions and your personal spite stand between your duty and a man's life. I don't give two damns if this man brushed you off, made false promises or even violated you in public. Your duty was plain and you failed in that duty."

"I am not refusing to go."

"Save your energy—a volunteer reported to this office exactly two minutes after the call. She is already well on her way."

"She!"

"Yes." Graham's lips almost smiled. "Miss Dunne—Miss Gina Dunne."

She flushed angrily but she said, calmly enough: "Director, as I understand it, this was a volunteer mission. I was not obliged to go."

"Irrespective of your personal prejudices, that is true. You were obliged, however, to report to my office immediately. You did not do so."

"Good God, I told you—I was asleep."

Graham sighed. "Miss Lane, I would advise you, between your emotional entanglements, to familiarize yourself with some of the subtleties of this base. Those emergency speakers are *special*. They are designed to penetrate the mind even if the hearer is in an exhausted sleep or deep sedation. Your excuse, therefore is not only a falsehood, but completely invalid."

He drew some papers closer to him and began to write. "I do not propose bringing you before a disciplinary board. You are young, you may learn better conduct and, when you put your mind to it, a brilliant biologist. I cannot let this breach of humanity and base discipline go unpunished, however. The emergency, and your deplorable part in it, will be written out in full and posted on all public notice boards."

He paused and looked up. "You have the right of appeal, of course, but a board of inquiry will take a dimmer view—"

IX

KILOMETERS AWAY, Ventnor was beginning to appreciate the insistence of haste. Already, after a bare twelve minutes walking, his thumb was black and the swelling had spread to the index finger and the palm of the hand. Furthermore his vision was becoming blurred and uncertain.

He stopped and thrust his spear into the soil. "R for Robert, reporting as instructed."

"You are three minutes late, Robert. Every *ten minutes!* We must keep a constant fix on your exact position. Describe the progress of your complaint, please."

He described it.

"Right, from here on take it easy. Double check your position every five minutes as you may become a little confused, but do not lose hope. Help is on its way—over and out."

Ventnor acknowledged the call and removed the spear from the soil. For some inexplicable reason the simple task required considerable effort. The damn spear seemed to have got blasted heavy suddenly.

Ten minutes later, however, it required even more effort to push it back again.

"Receiving you, Robert. How are you feeling?"

"Not an advertisement for physical training. My vision is

blurred, I'm getting periods of breathlessness and my whole hand is swollen."

"Acknowledged. During the periods of breathlessness, stand and rest. At the present stage they should be of only limited duration."

"You're doing a great job boosting my morale," said Ventnor sourly.

"Sorry, but you must understand you are a seriously sick man. If we are to get you back to base in one piece we cannot substitute unhelpful optimism for good advice."

"Sorry."

"Forget it, you're co-operating splendidly, keep it up."

Only fifteen minutes later, however, Ventnor had the curious feeling that the ground upon which he was walking was rolling like the deck of a ship. This produced a painful nausea which he had some difficulty in fighting down.

When it came time to report again it was almost beyond him. He was compelled to scoop a small hole in the ground with his good hand before he could make contact with the spear. When he finally succeeded, he fell over and couldn't get up.

He shouted thinly from the ground. "This is—Robert—can you hear me?"

"Receiving you, Robert."

"I've fallen over—I—can't get up."

"Stay where you are. Help is only minutes away."

"Under—stood." The sun had begun to dance crazily in the sky, making him feel sick. With some effort he rolled over but for some reason he couldn't explain the ground began to spin beneath him, threatening, so he thought, to send him sliding from the center to the ends of the earth.

He found a projection in the soil and clung to it desperately with his good hand.

He did not hear anyone arrive but a voice said, "Hold on, you're not alone now."

There were faint metallic sounds and something began to snip at his sleeve.

"Listen, darling, I am going to inject you in the upper arm. It will hurt like hell but under no circumstances are you to clutch or rub it—blink your eyes if you understand —good."

Something pricked his arm and, almost immediately, pain struck at him with terrifying force. It felt as if boiling lead had been dropped on his arm and was spreading through his veins.

"No!" A hand gripped his wrist and held it firmly.

He struggled but the grip on his wrist turned to a lock. "You must not move."

Move? His arm and shoulder were in the fire—were they crazy?

He had no idea Gina was with him but, strangely, he called her name twice before he lost consciousness.

He had no recollection of the nearest patrol arriving an hour later or the long journey back to base strapped in a stretcher. Neither was he a witness to the intense team work on arrival as skilled experts labored to save his life.

In point of fact, it was eight days before he regained consciousness and a further fifteen before he could take a rational interest in events.

"You've lost about a quarter of your normal weight but we managed to save your hand and arm." Culbertson managed to look both paternal and triumphant at the same time. "You'll have to take it damned easy for a couple of months—that is to say a couple of months *after* we get you out of here."

"Thank you for everything—what did I pick up?"

"One of the less pleasant of the new micro-organisms."

"Touché—which one?"

"Hartman's Virus, unpopularly known as Blue-burst."

"I'd like to read up on it."

Culbertson's eyes widened slightly. "Bit out of your line, isn't it? I understood you were all set for micro-engineering with a small blend of electronics."

"I was—I still am, but I have to know about this."

"All in good time, old chap. Perhaps, if you continue to improve, you may have some light taped entertainment within the week."

Ventnor sighed, suddenly sleepy. "You're the doctor, but don't run a closed shop on me. I shall be—after—you." He was asleep before Culbertson could reply.

By the end of the week, however, he was gaining weight and beginning to improve rapidly.

He got at Culbertson again. "About that information."

"Again!" The medical director was beginning to look vaguely hunted.

"Again! I have to know about this."

"As soon as I can arrange it." Culbertson was stalling, knew it and was uncomfortably aware that his patient knew it also. Later he reported the matter to Stein.

"He's making good progress but he keeps harping on this damn disease—he wants to read up on it."

Stein smiled and said, "Let him."

"Let him! God, Mr. Prone will cut out my heart. He's all set to launch the man into micro-robotics."

"Then he'll have to wait, won't he? In any case I'll have a word with Prone myself. In the meantime, let your patient have what he wants, the hard way. In short, let him take a course in biology during convalescence. He can go through the practical side when he's well again."

"Are you mad, Stein?" Culbertson sounded slightly short of breath.

Stein laughed. "I refuse to answer that on the grounds that it may incriminate me." Then, seriously: "I think I know what I'm doing. I know this man, I know how his mind works." He patted the director on the shoulder. "I shall look to you to back me. Tell him he can't plunge into a subject bang in the middle, that he must start at the bottom and work his way up. If he agrees, which he will, grant him every possible facility."

Culbertson opened his mouth and shut it again before he spoke. "Anything else—doctor?"

"Well, since you are so co-operative, yes. I think he might have a visitor now."

"You have one in mind of course."

"Naturally—Miss Dunne."

Culbertson looked at him, colored slightly and then his lips twitched. "Well, well, well, I always thought you psychs were detached but, my God, you're positively avuncular."

"My middle name is Cupid," said Stein, gently. "Didn't you know?" He walked away smiling.

"A visitor?"

"Er—ah—yes." Culbertson had the uncomfortable feeling that a certain coyness of manner was visible through his professional manners. "You are well enough now." He smiled. "This visitor saved your life so she has priority." He left the room rather hurriedly.

Ventnor put the book down, feeling vaguely ill at ease. What did one say to someone who— How could one really express thanks, sincere thanks?

When she came in, however, the feeling changed.

"Gina!" What the hell had he been worrying about? He reached out and took both her hands. "Thank you, and bless you."

"You're looking better than when I last saw you darling." She sounded matter-of-fact but she made no attempt to release her hands.

"Don't fence with me, Gina. I've had a lot of time to think—do you always call your patients 'darling'?"

"Professional assurance," she said quickly.

He laughed, then he said seriously. "Judith was jealous, jealous of you. She knew how I felt before I knew myself. I could *talk* to you. You were warm, real and I felt sort of at home with you. I used to stay and talk because—because—I didn't know it myself, Gina, but Judith did. When she accused me, I denied it but it got me thinking."

His grip on her hands tightened. "Gina—"

Far away, out in the Atlantic, Skeld, the section director said: "Come in." Then: "Yes, Mr. Hobart, what is it?"

Hobart cleared his throat nervously before speaking. "Well, sir, I don't know if this is important or not but I thought it should be brought to your notice. Er—it's about my great-grandfather, sir."

"Your great-grandfather!"

"Yes, I've been going through some of his notes and recordings—merely from curiosity, you understand, but I stumbled on an omission which has worried me quite a little."

"You're speaking in abstracts, Hobart. Kindly get to the point, I've a heavy schedule ahead of me."

"Yes, sir. The old man had a rather unique and, to my mind, dangerous machine. In his notes I can find no record

84

of him having turned it off—it was long-life, sir, and solar-powered. *It may still be running.*"

Skeld's sandy eyebrows rose slightly, then he pulled a note pad towards him. "This borders on fantasy, doesn't it? However, in order to satisfy my curiosity, to set your mind at rest, and more important, to save time, please anser my questions. Your great-grandfather's profession?"

"Primarily a biologist, sir, but he was also a physicist of some note."

"And this—er—machine?"

"As far as I can gather, sir, he believed he could effect the behaviour patterns of certain forms of insects, such as ants, by its use. According to his notes, he succeeded in increasing the intelligence of some of the lower mammals by its use but ran up against certain limitations in this field—his findings are in this recorder if you wish to study them."

"Later, Hobart, if I consider it relevant. In the meantime where was this experiment being conducted?"

"Back of beyond, sir,—the upper reaches of the Amazon."

"Curious site for a research laboratory was it not?"

"Not in view of his notes, sir. In the first place, there were certain releases of hard radiation involved which the authorities were disturbed about in congested areas. In the second place, and more to the point, whatever insect he had in mind abounded in the area."

"What was this insect?"

"I don't know, sir. He uses biological symbols to describe it."

"I see." Skeld made a note. "And what makes you think he forgot to deactivate this device."

"Because, sir, all notes—and there were sixty-three—conclude with the words 'experiment concluded, device switched off'. All, that is, except the *last one*, sir."

"Can you suggest any reason for this?"

"Several, sir. He had received an invitation to the Island but hung on for as long as possible to further his research. While hoping to conclude his work within the week, he suddenly realized that his fliers had only thirty hours 'life' left to them. He, therefore, had to pull out in a hell of a hurry leaving half his equipment behind."

"And so?"

"And so he arrived at the Island, together with his wife, only one week before the world tried to take the Island by naval power. In this engagement, as you know, the Island suffered only eight fatalities—unfortunately he was one of them." Hobart paused and shuffled his feet uncomfortably.

"You know how it is, sir. You have some spare time, you think: *I wonder what the old boy was up to*— It may be silly, sir, but I thought the matter should be brought to your attention."

Skeld nodded curtly. Hobart was obviously dreaming up things. On the other hand, a device with radiation leaks was not a sensible thing to leave around. "Very well, if you will give me the map co-ordinates, I will divert one of our regular weekly ships to the Rio villages."

When Hobart had gone, Skeld shrugged. Hadn't Hobart been punished for—no, not Hobart, the other fellow, Matheson. Yes, of course, that business over the escaped specimen.

Something in Skeld's mind seemed to click. Yes, the specimen, Ventnor—must be four or five years ago now. How time flew, been meaning to check that business but what with those tribes in Eastern Europe who had discovered a cache of machine guns somewhere. Then, of course, there had been that trouble on the coast of Maine. Fine thing when your own experimental villages rose in revolt. All because some fool of a yokel had dug up a couple of long-life books in a tin box while ploughing. All that trouble over a couple of books: *The History of the American Peoples* and *The Declaration of Independence*. A couple of books, what the hell!

His mind returned to the immediate problem and he spun the index dial of the file system. Almost immediately the open file appeared on the reader screen.

Skeld read it through carefully and frowned: "Existence of body confirmed by instruments but not by exhumation." He didn't care for that particularly—it was incomplete and, as such, was out of line with the traditions of the department. The body should have been exhumed at the time and the bone structure compared with the standard medical records of the deceased specimen.

86

Skeld called personnel. "Kindly assign me an expert from Medical Identification and a ship for a special mission."

Such was Skeld's authority that both were available within four hours and, after brief instructions were on their way.

The director did not expect them to find anything out of the ordinary but he detested loose ends. Incomplete confirmation was, in his opinion, a reflection of departmental inefficiency and as such . . .

Unaware that only a few kilometers away a ship was descending near Harthill Crossroads to check his 'remains' Ventnor was still with Gina.

The vessel was not, however, unobserved by others.

"They're not coming down there by accident, better let Graham know."

The base director, however, who liked to play things close to his chest, only smiled. "Let them search, they'll find enough soil impressions to confirm that the body was there but no body or remains. Taken them a long time to get here, hasn't it?"

When Skeld received the negative report, he frowned. One could expect little else really, too many carrion about and a shallow grave— Oh, well, his department had fulfilled its obligations, nothing to worry about, really.

Less than a week later, however, he was jolted out of his complacency. A panel in the wall of his room lit luridly— a class-5 alarm!

Skeld switched in to number five circuit and got the involved departments on his three dimensional screen. The emergency was in 'Flights' and it didn't take him more than six seconds to find out what was wrong—a ship was in trouble. An harassed-looking controller was giving quick but calm advice to the pilot.

"All right, R-9, open the emergency panel and pull the red switch, we'll push your emergency power out from here. What's your flying speed?"

Skeld did not hear the pilot's answer but he was dimly aware of a trickle of sweat crawling down his temple. R-9, that was the Rio ship—the ship he had diverted to check that Hobart business.

The controller was speaking again, this time sharply. "For

87

God's sake get a grip on yourself, Rennie, we're getting you back."

"At eighty-five flying kilometers an hour! Hasn't it sunk in yet? We were attacked! I'm a sitting duck up here, push some blasted speed into this kite, do you hear me?"

"Easy, old chap—"

"And you can skip the 'soothing-the-hysterical-patient' tone as well. Take a look at this ship."

Skeld found himself looking at a vibrating but still clear picture of the interior of R-9. In its sides were at least five jagged holes through which the wind was howling noisily. •

"See?" The pilot thrust his head close to the screen. "What do you think did that—moths?"

The controller took a deep audible breath. "If we push you any faster, the kite will fold up in the air—clear?"

"Okay." The pilot was calmer now but sullen. "Okay, you don't have to draw a diagram, frying pan or fire." Then, wearily: "Hooker is dead—he copped it just after we saw it."

"Saw what?" The controller's voice lacked curiosity, he was obviously more intent on keeping the pilot calm.

"The—the—" Rennie made a helpless movement with his shoulders. "God knows, it was like a lake of fine wire or spun glass, all running in spirals, like they used to lay barbed wire. We came in over a mountain and there it was, miles of it, glittering in the sun. We managed to get a couple of pictures and then Hooker fell backwards holding his chest —can't you turn this blasted kite towards the sea? *Must* you hold it over the land?"

Skeld waited for no more, he sent an emergency call to Committee.

By the time the battered flying vessel arrived, a yellow alert was in force and all scientific departments on an emergency footing.

Rennie, the pilot, was almost dragged from the plane, sedated to calm him, patted on the back and given a large brandy to make him feel at home. Then he was hurried in front of the Committee to tell his story.

Rennie had a retentive memory and original turn of phrase and he made the story vividly real:

"On leaving the Rio villages as instructed we fed the map references into the auto-pilot and let the kite fix the course and height herself.

"She fixed herself a nice comfortable twenty thou' to avoid any mountain tops which might get in the way and just aimed herself.

"About sixty kilometers from our destination, however, Hooker happened to glance down. I can remember his words clearly. He said: 'Looks as if someone has had a fire down there.'

"Naturally I had a look myself. Gentlemen, I don't mind admitting I was shaken. From horizon to horizon it was just green jungle steaming and shimmering in the heat but right below, covering about eighteen square kilometers, was a burned out patch. It was just as if the damp jumgle had been burned to the ground.

"We switched the kite to manual and went down to take a closer look but when we locked steady at a couple of meters it looked more like a battle ground. Everything was blackened as I said, but the ground was all rotting tree trunks, broken or burned off, and the ground was pitted with little holes like craters. It looked as if it had been that way a long time, perhaps ten years, but nothing grew.

"Funny thing was that the audio-geiger got hysterics as soon as we stopped. It kept switching on the alarm lights and bawling: 'Dangerous radiation. Do not leave vessel.'

"Hooker thought it might be out of order but rather than take chances, we stayed put and took soil samples with scoops. The auto-geiger didn't care for that either. 'Samples referred to safety holds,' it shouted. 'Radio-active material must not be approached.'

"We took several samples, quite a few from a muddy stream which ran through this burned area—all of it was 'hot.'

"After that we went on and—"

It was then that Pressly called from the biological laboratories. He was pale and sweating visibly. "Take a look at *this*," he said. . . .

89

X

THEY LOOKED. They looked at the screen, at Pressly in it, they looked at the photograph he held in his hand and they looked at each.

Finally a Committee member said: "You'd better come up here."

Pressly got there so quickly that wondering comment had barely begun and immediately he cut it short.

"This frightens me to death." He thrust the photograph into the room projector, flicked the switch and stood glowering nervously while it warmed. A tall, pale man with a jutting, pointed chin and thick black eyebrows which he never bothered to trim, he had not bothered to remove his laboratory coat and clearly he was as alarmed as he claimed.

Finally the picture appeared on the wall screen and they stared at it uncomprehendingly.

"This came up with some of the samples," he said. "Presumably one of those selected from the stream."

"You mean this photograph came up with the samples?" The questioner sounded puzzled and completely out of his depth.

Pressly, noted for his quick temper and his biting sarcasm, turned a dull red.

"Is my command of this language so grossly inadequate or are you being deliberately obtuse, sir? *This*—must I define the word?—came up with one of the samples. The photograph, I repeat, the photograph itself, is ours and was taken with a biological camera. In short gentlemen, the object you are observing *is almost as small as a non-filterable virus.*"

They stared, as if by their staring they could make the picture disappear. All were aware of disbelief and a cold feeling of apprehension inside them. Some of the more intelligent however, were already cursing themselves for not noticing details.

The picture itself, at first glance, might have been one of thousands taken in the World War II, until one studied the design, the application, the wholly alien in a horribly familiar implication. *It couldn't be—could it?*

90

The picture showed a curiously shaped vessel with a hole in its side. Fixed to the vessel's flat deck were six tracked objects. The bows of the vessel which carried them had been lowered to form a ramp.

It was impossible to say whether the vessel had been designed to fly, float on water or travel in some other medium, but its purpose was obvious—*it was a tank landing craft*.

Most of the members became aware of an icy prickling at the backs of their necks. You couldn't conceive of L.C.T. that small could you?

Slowly their eyes turned from the photograph and back to Pressly. Eyes filled with disbelief, anger, fear, rank rejection and not a few with a kind of anguished hope. Maybe Pressly would explain it away, tell them there was nothing to worry about.

Pressly didn't. His next few words tore not only the hopes but all the other emotions into tiny meaningless shreds.

He removed something from his pocket, his thick black eyebrows moving curiously. "I have here a complete report from the Department of Physicists." He looked at them directly. "The blackened area is 'hot', radio-active from end to end. The radio-activity is on the decline, but the department concerned has confirmed by test that this activity dates back some thirty odd years."

He paused and looked at them again. "How many *relative* years is that, gentlemen, a thousand—ten thousand. How many generations of God-knows-what?"

He paused, sensing the scepticism. "Gentlemen, when I have finished, and at your convenience, you may visit the laboratories and check the evidence. This vessel you are observing in the photograph is not the only sub-microscopic artifact we found by any means. You are just seeing the best photograph.

"The physicists among you may make your own checks but you will arrive at the same answer."

He paused and thrust another photograph into the viewer. "This is the area of devastation viewed from the damaged aircraft. Make no mistake, gentlemen, thirty years ago something fought a war here and they fought it with hydro-nuclear devices. In all probability the 'mushrooms' of these devices seldom rose higher than a normal mushroom, a few centimeters, barely the height of a man's ankle but they were released in such great numbers that they completely obliterated this area of jungle. An area, which I may add, would hold the cities of London and greater New York at the height of their glory. Something—some intelligence—so small that our imagination veers away from the conception."

He paused again and went on in a strangely subdued voice. "Gentlemen, you are entitled to scepticism, it is your right to theorize, but the fact that troubles us most, is the unavoidable conclusion that this intelligence is not only still alive but aware of our existence as a possible threat. . . ."

In Base 4, Ventnor, now fully recovered, was already formidably fortified by advanced courses in practical biology.

"This particular organism, Mr. Ventnor, should be of considerable interest to you personally—Hartman's Disease."

Ventnor studied it. Through the magnifier, it resembled a piece of black cotton, a centimeter or so in length. "Not a lot to work on, is there?"

"Unfortunately we have reached the limits of sub-microscopic magnification. The device to bring that culture any closer has yet to be invented."

"What are the exact effects on the human body?"

"Directly and simply, it attacks the nerve membranes. Indirectly, in the normal functions of its existence, it excretes toxics which effect the blood. The life cycle of the organism is short but the rate of reproduction fantastic. In your case, for example, another thirty minutes would have been too late."

"What methods do you employ to combat the virus?"

"In the human body, a twofold method. A special antibiotic which attacks the virus directly and a substance to cleanse the bloodstream of the toxic by-products of the disease."

Ventnor said, "I see," and scowled.

Later that day, with Gina, he was absent-minded and a little vague.

She was not troubled. She understood, loved him and knew he had a problem on his mind.

Finally he said: "I have an idea, I think it might work."

92

Then, irrelevantly, "You have the most gentle brown eyes I have ever seen, gentle and understanding."

"Does that help your ideas?" She was smiling gently.

"Yes, it does, I feel at peace with you. Your eyes are part of that peace, part of you." Suddenly he took her in his arms. "I love you."

"I know." Her arms went round his neck.

He kissed her again. "I don't feel peaceful now."

"I know that, too."

"Darling, will you marry me—?"

"Later." She drew his mouth down to hers. "Later, when you— Oh, darling—feel—peaceful again—"

Three weeks later he called Biology.

"Where the hell have you been?" Latimer's thin face was slightly flushed.

"Working—sorry, should have let you know but I got so involved. Listen, you told me that a device to magnify Hartman's Disease had yet to be invented—magnify it any more, that is." Ventnor drew a deep breath, clearly he was excited.

"Very well, go on." Latimer sounded resigned.

"Go on? Oh, sorry—er—I think I've invented it."

"The hell you have! Where are you?"

"Department C—can you bring some culture along?"

"Bring some—" Latimer hesitated. "It will have to be latent, you know, sterile, the rules forbid— Be with you in about six minutes."

Fifteen minutes later, Latimer's mouth opened but no sound came out.

The virus which, with his instruments, had looked like a centimeter of black cotton, now looked like an untidy piece of rope. It was, or appeared to be, nearly a meter long and was as thick as a man's arm.

"How the hell did you do it?"

"Later, if you don't mind. Apart from known methods, if it were alive what would kill it?"

"I don't quite follow you."

"You don't have to—yet. I was thinking of a heavy electrical discharge."

Latimer, uncomfortably aware that he was getting out of

93

depth in his own field of research, said tartly, "Most certainly, but the patient would go with it."

"Not if it were a constricted discharge, electronically confined to the nervous system of the virus."

"What do you propose to do—jump into the patient's blood stream and pick them off like a sniper?"

Ventnor's mouth twitched slightly, then he said, "Yes," with a straight face.

For a few moments he watched the changing expressions on Latimer's face then he held out his hand. "Sorry, Mr. Latimer, I've a warped sense of humor. Come and see what I'm working on."

Latimer tried to frown disapprovingly and failed. Ventnor was one of the most infuriating and, at the same time, one of the most likeable men he had ever met.

"Very well." He followed meekly.

Thirty minutes later, however, he had the uncomfortable feeling that his eyes were bulging slightly.

"It can't be done, Ventnor, truly it cannot be done." Latimer made the statement almost defensively. The other's conceptions were so incredibly unorthodox that its very existence threatened to undermine the techniques both of biology and preventative medicine at a single stroke.

"Why can't it be done? You, yourself, told me that medical science can now educate the normal metabolism into accepting certain substances."

"Well—because—" Latimer, now flushed and scowling was horrified to discover that he couldn't think of a reason, not at the moment, not off hand. "It would have to be tried on a live culture first."

"Naturally."

"It will have to be examined by a panel of experts."

"Of course, I expect that."

Latimer almost shook his fist. "Will you please stop being so infuriatingly submissive. You're not even giving me the satisfaction of an argument. Damn it, man, this has been a shock."

When, subsequently, the matter was examined by a panel of experts, only two stubbornly refused to be shocked.

Stein only smiled blandly as if he had expected it and Prone was noisily jubilant.

94

"Didn't I tell you? Didn't I say he'd turn up something good?"

"The device has yet to be tested, Mr. Prone," said one of the experts a little tartly.

"Isn't that why we are here?"

"But, of course—"

"Then kindly refrain from holding up the proceedings with veiled sarcasms."

The device was tested and there were gasps of almost indignant disbelief. A conception like this *couldn't* work, yet they were watching it.

Only Ventnor was vaguely dissatisfied. "The materials employed, by their very nature, are short-life. We need a substance, possibly a plastic, atomically arranged, both for durability and strength in those conditions."

Prone looked at Walman of Plastics and said: "Well?"

Surprisingly Walman smiled. "It's going to be tough but I like a challenge. I'm going to need the co-operation of a top rate physicist, however."

Within four days, both departments were working at full pressure and coming up with some promising substances. At the end of the week they had it and Ventnor went in for the equivalent of mass production.

Passing along the corridor a day later, however, he ran into Judith. It was the first time he had seen her since their parting some months before and he reddened uncomfortably.

"Hello, Judith."

Her eyes widened and she stopped dead. "Did you say something—please?"

"Yes, I said 'hello'."

"*You* spoke to *me?*" She sounded choked.

"Why, yes—shouldn't I?"

"I—I—" Suddenly her eyes filled with tears. "No one speaks to me. My name is on the notice board, didn't you know?"

"Yes, I knew but no one tells me to whom I should speak or should not speak."

She said, almost angrily: "Indirectly I tried to kill you,

95

deliberately I tried to kill you. I hated you, don't you understand that?"

"Of course I understand it, Judith. It happened, it's over and, as far as I am concerned, done with."

She shook her head in a puzzled way. "Why you, why should you speak, you had the least reason." She averted her face slightly. "You must be a very kind man—I don't think, until now, I ever really understood kindness. I always regarded it as sentimentality without depth—a form of weakness."

He said, "You're not looking well, Judith."

"You're trying to spare me embarrassment, aren't you? The need to say what I should say, that I'm sorry. It's too late now but I am sorry, Robert, not only sorry for what it brought me but sorry for—do you forgive me?"

He smiled gently. "I said it was done with and you still look unwell."

"I have my off days, forget it." She turned quickly. "Thank you, Robert, see you again, perhaps—"

Later, with Gina, he was troubled and she was quick to notice.

"Tell me about it."

He smiled. "We really don't have to talk, do we? You know without me telling you." He stroked her cheek with his fingertips. "You're a very wonderful women." He was suddenly worried again. "I met Judith this morning—Gina, I don't know for certain but I think she's got *Metricitus.*"

She sat upright. "Then you must call section 7."

He nodded. "I could be mistaken, but we did happen to touch on it in biology. There was the characteristic expansion of the pupils and her hair looked kind of limp."

She laid her hand on his arm. "Call the section."

"It's not because I still feel anything for her. I love you."

"My darling, I *know* that."

"You're wonderful, Gina." He touched the caller. "Section 7, please."

The medico at the other end heard him out. "Well, of course, it was your duty to report it but it's a very rare disease you know—who did you say it was?" He listened and said: "Oh, her!"

Ventnor flushed. "Miss Lane, whatever happened in the

96

past, has the same medical rights as anyone else on the base."

"All right, calm down, we'll pull her in for a checkup right away."

An hour later, however, Culbertson himself called. "Thank you for your call to this section—" He hesitated. "I'm afraid we got a positive count."

"Good God—how?"

"Well, we found a microscopic scratch on the third finger of her right hand. She wouldn't have noticed it at the time. Later we found traces of the virus in one of the samples she was working on. There's no cause for alarm, the disease as you know, enters the body through a wound. We have taken all the necessary sterilization precautions."

"Have you caught it in time?"

"It's too early to say."

"That means you haven't."

"I did not say that, Mr. Ventnor. She must have contracted the disease only a few hours after her last medical so that it had a week to gain a hold."

"You know damn well what that means."

"I assure you that everything possible is being done."

"I believe that without your assurance—thank you for calling me." He broke contact.

"Gina, she's going to die. She'll lie there for four months getting thinner and weaker. It's one of the new complaints, kind of a muscular tuberculosis ending in total paralysis."

She looked up into his face. "Bob, darling, what is it?"

He looked at her and away. "Gina, I've cooked up something—it's what I've been working on—it could save her. On the other hand it's not been tested properly and might very well kill her."

She took his hand. "You've got to try."

He smiled her twistedly. "If they'll let me."

They didn't let him. They were polite but firm although, unknown to him, their refusal sparked off one of the biggest departmental rows since the inception of the base.

"I don't care who you are, Mr. Graham." Culbertson's face was flushed. "You have no jurisdiction over my department in this matter."

"I am not trying to run your department at all, Mr.

Culbertson. I am merely trying to put another point of view. The girl is going to die, isn't she?"

Culbertson looked sullen. "The odds are against her, yes."

"Can you offer a fifty-fifty chance of survival?"

"Not today, perhaps tomorrow."

"Damn tomorrow, would this technique save her?"

"For the hundredth time, I don't know. It's only been tested in a culture tray. One thing I do know, however, it might kill her—suppose it does kill her. Think about that, then next day, perhaps, someone comes up with something which we *know* would have saved her. Would you want that on *your* conscience, Mr. Graham?"

"No, I wouldn't. Neither will I like it, if by ignoring a possible method, the girl is allowed to die."

"You're trying to dictate to me again, sir. Do you think I haven't thought of that too."

"Of course you've thought of it, Mr. Culbertson and, like myself you're not a hundred per cent sure you're right." He looked at the other directly. "I respect both your principles and your ethics. I like you as a man and I cannot speak too highly of your work here. Despite this, however, I am afraid I have to go over your head—I propose referring this matter to the International Medical Council."

Strangely, Culbertson said, "Thank you." He lowered himself into the nearest chair. "Sooner or later I suppose I should have done that myself—yes, I'm not sure but while I carried the responsibility I had to act as I saw fit."

"And I respect you for it." Graham leaned back in his chair and smiled tiredly. "I suppose in a way my conscience was pricking me also. You see, although Miss Lane's conduct was inexcusable, it was I who imposed her punishment. Had she been mixing with her colleagues in a normal manner her complaint would have been spotted sooner and, perhaps treated in time."

Less than six hours later, the first call came: "This is the French sector of Association. We have received your report together with certain reservations—is the patient aware both of the nature of her complaint and its outcome?"

"The patient is a biologist; she has no illusions."

"That is not enough. The patient must not only be advised of her condition but the methods to be employed fully explained to her. If you are prepared to assure us on this point you may accept our reply as in the affirmative."

"You have my assurance."

After that Graham received three uncompromising negatives. Less than an hour later, however, he had five affirmatives. The last, surprisingly, came from Germany and was almost Gaelic in its enthusiasm. "Our sector regards this as a break-through of no mean order. Even, in the unhappy event of it proving unsuccessful in these circumstances, the possibilities are limitless."

The United States was almost equally enthusiastic but raised the same point as the French sector—the patient must be told and, in the event of a tie, given the deciding vote.

About the middle of the following day, Culbertson called on Ventnor personally.

"Well, you're on." He held out his hand. "Although I deplore the result personally, I wish you the very best of luck. No hard feelings?"

XI

SHE LAY IN the narrow bed, no longer full-figured and voluptuous but thin, pale and very tired.

He said, diffidently. "I've brought Gina with me, I hope you don't mind."

She smiled faintly. "Mind? Truly I wish you every happiness. Let's face it, I was a bitch."

"We're being televised, Judith."

"I was still a bitch, Robert. It's a mercy I know it at last."

"You know why I have come? They've told you a little?"

"A little—you have some new technique which may cure or kill. I'm prepared to take a chance. I know what I've got." She sighed. "No good saying I'm not frightened, particularly so as the mind remains clear and lucid to the last."

Strangely she smiled and looked up at him. "You're scared too."

He nodded quickly and said, "I have to explain the techniques employed, not only to give you the right to refuse but for the benefit of all those who are watching—you're not too tired?"

99

"No, I'm wide awake, another aspect of the disease, one gets very little sleep."

"Very well, Judith, let's begin." He held up a photograph. "You will remember this—a picture of Hartman's virus taken with the then-existing techniques."

He paused and produced another photograph. "The same virus taken by new methods." He drew a deep breath and hurried on, conscious that his voice was quavering slightly.

"I'll tell you how it was done. I constructed a micro-robotic and programed it to build another micro-robotic ten times smaller than the original. The second micro-robotic was equipped with a tele-camera. I photographed the virus, beamed the picture back to the first one which in turn beamed it back to existing equipment—follow me?"

She nodded. "I wish I'd had equipment like that."

"Never mind that now." He was almost brusque and his hands were shaking so much that he was compelled to signal an orderly to bring the remaining equipment to the table.

He cleared his throat quickly. "This black box here, believe it or not, is a micro-robotic auto-factory designed to mass produce parts, program tapes for the monitors and micro-robotic workers which, in turn, produced this." He pointed to small object exactly similar. "As you see, it has been reduced to the size of the ancient match box."

He paused and cleared his throat nervously again. "This second auto-factory produces micro-biotics of a special nature."

He paused again and said, almost calmly: "I must digress here to pay proper tribute to the experts both in plastic and in nuclear physics whose work made the construction of these sub-microscopic robots possible. It was they alone who came up with durable substances capable of being molded to these conditions."

He turned again to the objects on the table and pointed to the smallest black box. "This auto-factory has one task—mass-producing *these*."

The far wall of the room lit suddenly and the viewers saw a curious gray pear-shaped object with a tube at the thicker end.

"This object, strictly speaking, is a constructed micro-organism about the size of Hartman's virus. It is molded from special plastics, the molecules of which have been atomically arranged for durability in these conditions."

He paused and almost managed a smile. "It is also a warrior robot."

Again he paused and drew a deep audible breath. "Impressed on the recognition tapes of this robot is a picture of the *Metricitus spirochaeta!*"

He walked over to the picture and pointed. "This pointed tube at the front of the robot is a contact device. It is designed to release on contact with the spirochaeta a lethal charge of electricity electronically restricted to a nervous system, or it you prefer it, the substance of the hostile micro-organism."

He turned to Judith and said, gently, "Have you followed me?"

"Yes, I've followed you." She looked puzzled.

"Judith, this auto-factory has produced sub-microscopic robots in hundred of millions. I propose injecting a few million into your blood stream in a special solution and letting them seek out and destroy the spirochaeta which are causing your illness. This method has been tested and proved in an infected culture but never in a living organism —do you fully understand me?"

She nodded, very slowly. "Yes—yes, I understand you." Then, thoughtfully: "It's a gamble, isn't it? If nothing is done I shall die anyway—go ahead, what have I got to lose?"

"Thank you, Judith—for trusting me." He made a brief signal with his hand and Latimer entered from an open side door almost immediately.

"Are you quite sure, Judith?"

"Quite, Mr. Latimer."

"Very well. I am now going to inject you in the upper arm but I must warn you in advance not to expect miracles."

He inserted the needle skillfully and continued: "You will not rise from your bed in half an hour and do a war dance. In fact it is very doubtful if you will be aware of any change at all for at least a week.

"These micro-robotics have an effective life of only six

101

hours, after which they dissolve into harmless substances and are disposed of by the body.

"Every six hours, therefore, I shall have to introduce another host of fighters into your bloodstream to keep up the good work. This alone will not spell your recovery but it should reduce the numbers of hostile organisms to controllable limits. Once this is achieved orthodox medicine and the natural reflexes of the body should prove decisive."

He patted her shoulder and smiled. "Would you like to see what is going on? Look at the wall facing your bed."

The wall faded, became a vague outline which hardened slowly into a tunnel. A murky tunnel in which half-visible shapes moved sluggishly like thick and muddy water.

"Not a very clear picture, is it? It is the interior of one of your veins—ah, that's a little better."

It was more than better. Although it still looked vague and muddled, experts among the watchers could clearly distinguish the red and white corpuscles.

"Ah! One of your uninvited guests." Latimer's voice cracked a little with excitement. "See it? That thing like a coiled spring, up on the left there, half-embedded in the wall of the vein. Keep your eyes on it as one of the microscopic robots may have detected it, a limited number are equipped with tele-cameras for just that purpose."

As he spoke the picture seemed to split in two, one half concentrating on the spirochaeta and the other illumination the now familiar pear-shaped micro-robotic. This drifted almost lazily with the bloodstream, then, when it was almost level with the spirochaeta, stopped.

It turned with almost painful slowness then appeared to jet itself abruptly at its target.

Nothing spectacular happened. The tube of the micro-robotic touched briefly and then it allowed itself to be carried away.

After a brief period, however, the spirochaeta appeared to go limp. It was ejected from, or could not hold itself to, the wall of the vein and drifted away from it.

The picture was maintained long enough for the viewers to see it run into a white corpuscle which immediately began to absorb it.

As the picture disappeared, Latimer said, "My God, it's really *working!*"

Judith looked up at Ventnor, there was a glimmer of hope in her eyes. "If it works, I don't deserve it."

"Don't say that, everyone has the right to live."

"I tried to deny you that right."

He made an almost angry gesture. "Not now, Judith! Let us both pray that it works."

Later that day he said to Gina, "If it fails, I've betrayed her. I've used her as a guinea pig to prove a theory."

"No, my darling, no—come and sit down." She put her arms round his neck. "Rest, you're tired and over-wrought."

He smiled twistedly. "I'm going to stay that way for at least a week. . . ."

Had he known what was going on far out in the Atlantic he would have been even more over-wrought.

Kerenski, an expert, tossed a small stone on Skeld's desk. "I've had that on a dozen instruments, it's 'live'."

"What do you mean by that?"

"It's a normal stone brought back in a soil sample from the alleged grave of your specimen, Robert Ventnor."

"Get to the point." Skeld was harsh. He had a lot on his mind.

"Very well, this stone is giving off the 'personality aura' of this supposedly deceased specimen with almost the same strength as if he were still alive."

Skeld paled. "What do you conclude from that?"

Kerenski smiled without humor. "Well, he could have been buried alive for five years which is absurd. Alternatively, he could have been alive all the time and sat on his own grave for about an hour just before we investigated. No, the only conclusion, and a frightening one, is that a device was placed in the grave to simulate a personality aura. Unfortunately this stone was near it and, unlike the soil, retained the emanations from this device."

Skeld half rose from behind his desk. "But that presupposes an advanced technology."

"It presupposes nothing, Mr. Skeld, it *confirms* an advanced technology."

Skeld lowered himself slowly into his chair, his mind racing. The Maidstone boys, massed cross-bows, unarmed combat, things that gave them an edge over local tribes without arousing undue suspicion. It could be—was—a 'front', a disguise, an ingenious masquerade.

He said, in a calm voice, "Thank you, Mr. Kerenski. I will draw the attention of the Committee to your excellent work in this matter." He made a gesture of dismissal. "You may leave this with me."

When Kerenski had gone, however, Skeld was aware of an uneasy fluttering in his stomach. Hadn't they enough trouble? One hundred and sixty-three probes sent to the South American trouble spot and every one blown to pieces in the sky. Now this! Skeld shivered—an impossible situation of limitless danger which could be laid directly at the door of his department. Slackness! Incompetence! The words seemed to dance slowly and heavily in his mind.

No, he had to handle this himself—fast, and with the minimum of publicity.

He made a call. "Send Mr. Hobart to my office immediately."

His instructions to Hobart, when he arrived, were amiable in tone but contained a kernel of threat. "You will appreciate that had I phrased your report in less favorable terms, you would have found yourself in trouble—this South American business is bad you know."

When he had finished, Hobart was not only pale but anxious to ingratiate himself. Skeld threw in the department's good name and Hobart's precarious position in it as added weight before he gave his instructions.

"Seems simple enough, sir."

"Good, good— Oh, and yes, Hobart, take Matheson with you. After all, this entire situation could be due to his small but vital delay. Give him the chance to make amends, as it were. Not a satisfying character, our Mr. Matheson— weakly sentimental, lacks the scientific approach—don't you agree?"

Hobart said he agreed entirely.

An hour later he and Matheson were on their way, the Island falling away below them.

Hobart looked down at it. "Still gives me a kick," he said.

"When I stop and think that man built that. An island as big as a continent—the peak of civilization."

Matheson shook his head tiredly. "Civilization is hooped together, brought under a semblance of peace by manifold illusion."

"Eh?" Hobart looked puzzled, then frowned. "You're quoting at me again," he accused.

"Not at you, just quoting. There was a great deal of wisdom in the past."

"Wisdom or whimsy?"

"A matter of opinion. Care to hear the rest?"

"Not in the least, we have a job to do, clearing up some unfinished business—*your* unfinished business."

"What the hell are you talking about?"

Hobart told him.

"So he may have got away. Good luck to him."

Hobart scowled at him. As Skeld had observed, Matheson was not a satisfying character—not that he had anything against him personally. He was amiable, too amiable, perhaps, but quite useful in minor ways, like changing shifts and things like that. On the other hand, as Skeld said, he was weak, sentimental, a born do-gooder. All those books he read, philosophy, verse, took no interest at all in competitive sport or the true scientific approach. If the Island was ever in danger and Matheson came face to face with a fight, he'd fold up before a shot was fired.

"Where are we going anyway?" Matheson sounded disinterested.

Hobart smiled. This was going to be the test, this was going to show just how weak Matheson was. "I told you, we're going to clear up some of your unfinished business —we're going to get the specimen once and for all. Mr. Skeld is of the opinion, as I believe I mentioned, that he was picked up by the Maidstone boys and is probably still with them."

"You did! What about it?"

"I'm afraid, to get him, we'll have to get the lot."

"How do you propose to do that?"

Hobart pointed a freckled finger at the release stud. "With that. In the bomb bay is a little cylinder all ready for me to press that button—only I'm not going to press

105

it—you are." He smiled unpleasantly. "I'm not attached to the Department Of Bacterialogical Warfare so I can't tell you the exact contents of the cylinder. All I know is that it contains a virus, highly contagious but with a restricted life of only forty-eight hours. There is no danger, therefore, of it spreading to other tribes. This lot, however, and to quote an ancient cliché, will go down like corn before a scythe."

He paused, smiling at the other's stricken face. "Something the matter, old chap."

Matheson shook his head. "I thought you said these people had technology. If they have"—his voice rose suddenly—"there is only one conclusion. Their ancestors stayed behind to keep civilization going when ours were running like rats for the Island."

Hobart flushed angrily. "Any damn thing to bolster your cloying sentimentality."

"I'm not pressing that damn button for you, Skeld, or the entire Committee."

"Let us not become hysterical, eh? I never thought you would. I shall press it, of course."

"If you move your finger one centimeter towards that button I shall blow off your entire hand without a second thought."

Hobart stiffened and turned slowly. "Really, Matheson, there are limits even to your—" His mouth fell open idiotically. "P—p—put that gun away, you damn fool."

"When you move away from that stud."

"Now look, use your head, I'm flying this kite."

"Not any more—switch in the auto-pilot."

"Matheson, they'll shoot you for this." He pulled the appropriate switch. "You must have gone mad." He half rose.

"I wouldn't!" Matheson took a step forward and swung the gun, butt first.

Hobart sat suddenly back, swayed uncertainly, then rolled out of it onto the floor.

Matheson leaned over and removed the regulation side-arm from the other's holster, then he waited.

After a short time Hobart opened his eyes and blinked at the floor. Then he struggled to a sitting position and held his head. There was a deep cut and an ugly spreading bruise on his temple. He put his hand to it and winced.

Matheson! Matheson had done this—hit him, hit him hard—namby-pamby Matheson!

"You could have killed me," he said thickly.

"One false move, one single attempt to drop that cylinder, and I shall."

Hobart staggered unsteadily to his feet and leaned against the wall. "You—you *mean* it." The gun pointing at his stomach was frighteningly steady. "You actually mean it."

"You don't know how much I mean it. You don't know what it means to live your life in a mental vacuum and suddenly come up against a clear decision which you *know* is right."

Hobart smiled uneasily. "Take it easy, old chap, you're not *thinking*. You're only postponing the inevitable. Furthermore you'll never get away with it. In the first place, you must either stay here or you must go back. If you go back, they'll execute you; if you stay here you'll either starve to death or they'll blow us both to bits."

He smiled again, this time with almost convincing friendliness. "Now be reasonable, give me the gun and no one will be any the wiser. This is an incident which is best forgotten and you can rely on me never to say a word about it. Come on now, give me the gun."

Matheson showed his teeth. It was not a smile. "I get the strong impression that you think you're humoring a lunatic. For God's sake, *grow up*, Hobart."

"Grow up? I don't know what you mean."

"I didn't think you did despite your constant reminders of the 'scientific approach' and your pathetic adulation of Island civilization."

Despite the gun, Hobart flushed angrily. "Watch what you're saying."

"I intend to, irrespective of the fact that it doesn't matter now. Item—and I have checked the figures—at the time of the collapse, the Island was producing a considerable surplus of synthetic foodstuffs. It was producing enough—and could have produced more—to provide salvation rations for the entire world. Not enough to provide four meals a day it is true but enough to ward off starvation."

107

He paused and jerked the gun meaningly. "Did it? Give the scientific answer, Hobart, did it?"

"Now look, there were a lot of considerations—"

"Yes or no, Hobart?"

The other scowled, looked at the gun and said: "No," sullenly.

"Quite, it sat on its collective backside and let the world slide to ruin—is that what you're so damn proud of?"

"We're trying to found a stable and sane society now," said Hobart defensively.

"By playing God? Don't make me laugh. Two hundred and seventy-five million guinea pigs genetically manipulated and psychologically coerced into what you hope will one day be a stable society. You, and a large number of Islanders like you, think you're omnipotent. You justify murder, semi-literacy, false premises and barefaced oppression on the grounds of scientific necessity. You're paranoics to a man, self-appointed demi-gods, inbred smug-uglies."

"Now watch it!" Hobart took an angry step forward.

The barrel of the gun jerked suddenly into his belly and he folded over with a gasp.

"I warned you, my friend. I must remind you also that I am being merciful, far more merciful than you have ever been to your innocent specimens or the tribes you keep alive for comparison purposes."

He stood back as the other straightened, wheezing. "Get your breath, my friend. I am even prepared to grant you some limited justice. If you can prove to me by science, logic, data or proven fact that anything I have said is untrue, I will not only return the gun but I will go back with you as your prisoner."

Hobart's mouth opened, the muscles of his face twitched but he only said: "Very slick, I suppose you think you have all the answers."

"No answers, only questions."

Hobart made an angry frustrated gesture. "All right, all right, you're a smart talker with a neat argument. If it's any satisfaction I'll concede defeat, but where does it get us?"

"It gets you nowhere but it gets me out from under my conscience."

"What do you intend to do—kill me and run?"

"And sink to your level of expedience? No, my friend. I propose switching on the audio-beam, calling down there to let them know what goes on and putting the ship down to meet them."

"You're mad. They'll kill us out of hand."

"Have you any proof of that? If these people are the descendants of those who remained behind, their ethics are probably superior to the sewer-level of Island morality."

"I'm remembering all this," said Hobart, thickly. "One day I hope I get the chance of beating in your damned head for all you've said."

"Of course. Beating in my head would be a far simpler solution to the problem than disproving my words—that is the scientific approach?"

Hobart shouted: "Blast you!" and turned his back on him.

"Stay that way." Matheson, still pointing the gun, switched on the audio-beam. "Hello, down there. . . ."

Those below were not surprised by the call. The ship had been tracked from the Island and, as soon as its course became apparent, linked for sound.

The entire conversation had been received by a increasing and frankly delighted audience of listeners far below the ground.

XII

THE DISAPPEARANCE of the flyer was not reported to Skeld for nearly eight hours.

"You took your damn time, didn't you?"

"Sorry, sir, we had to be certain. There have been occasions in which communications have failed."

"And this is not one of them?"

"Unfortunately, no. We have special equipment for getting a fix on a power-unit, even a dead one. As far as we are concerned, the ship and the two men in it have ceased to exist to normal methods of detection."

"I see. Thank you." Skeld broke contact, conscious of a

dampness on his forehead. He'd have to report this, the whole sorry business in complete detail. This was going to be big and very unpleasant for himself and the entire department.

Five hours later he was facing the highest court on the Island.

They heard him tell the entire story without comment which infused the entire proceedings with a detached and frightening coldness.

Finally, Loom, the President, leaned back in his chair and seemed to see Skeld for the first time. He did not, however, address him directly.

"We could describe this sorry story as 'the insolence of office', gentlemen. A fifth-rate executive acting ill-advisedly on his limited initiative and, in so doing, creating a unique niche for himself in the realms of general incompetence. Not content with this, he sacrifices two lives and an aircraft in desperate attempt to cover his mistakes."

There were nods and murmurs of agreement and Skeld had the uncomfortable feeling he was shrinking visibly. The President in his black robes in the high ornate chair seemed to glower down at him like some huge avenging eagle.

Skeld thought, in a brief inconsequential moment, that the simile was true. Loom had huge, slightly bowed shoulders, bushy white eyebrows and a large hooked nose.

"Gentlemen"—the President folded the fingers of his huge white hands one within another like a slowly closing trap—"despite the urgent need of bringing this incompetent before an examining board, the story he has told us must be our first consideration. Clearly we are faced with an advanced technology which, with singular insolence, has not only seen fit to conceal itself on our very doorstep but has had the temerity to intrude on our vital work.

"There can be no doubt in our minds as to procedure—this band of uncontrolled and dangerous Gadgeteers must be found and eliminated to a man."

It was then that the air seemed to crackle curiously and a pleasant, slightly amused voice said: *"Which band—ours or the seven thousand five hundred other bands dotted all over the world?"*

110

There was a pause and the committee members looked at each other disbelieving and almost accusingly. All their faces asked the same question—*who the hell said that?*

The voice answered obligingly. "One of the 'bands' said it. If you are interested, gentlemen, we can not only hear every word you say but see you as well—not bad for a Gadgeteer, would you say? However, to get down to basics, hadn't you better think again. You go gunning for that band on your doorstep and the rest of us will come gunning for you—clear?"

Again the voice paused. "We don't want war, gentlemen, but we'll fight if you force it on us. What we are seeking is the co-operation of all humanity to reclaim and rebuild the world, not two warring factions making it worse than it is already. Of course, being what you are, you may decide to fight, but if you do you'll go down in history as the greatest military incompetents the world has ever seen. A war on two fronts with the technical accomplishments and the potential strength of both factions a complete enigma—yes, we know about the South American business."

There was an amused laugh. "We have a comedian in our band now, joined us quite recently. He referred to you as an Island of smug-uglies—are you going to prove him right?"

There was a crackling sound again and the voice stopped. Within an hour, however, it was back but this time it spoke to the entire Island.

"Do you wish for a war on two fronts? Do you wish to cross swords with a sub-microscopic life-form more intelligent than yourselves? Do you, at the same time, hope to launch a punitive assault on your own kind? Are you strong enough for this kind of lunacy? Have you, for example, a clue to the potential of your human opponents, numerically, industrially or technically?"

The voice paused. "In all communities, there are the good and the bad, the sane and the insane, the reasoning and the unreasoning. Our appeal is to the sane, the good, the reasoning. It is an appeal to unite with us to rebuild the world, to reclaim the heritage of all humanity."

By this time, nearly the entire electronic resources and

technical wizardry of the Island were concentrated on tracing the source of the broadcast.

Harassed technicians and experts with angry executives breathing down their necks labored desperately to obtain a fix with infuriatingly abortive results.

The first three words came from Central Germany, the next three on a different frequency, came from the United States, the next three from Australia and so on. Yet there was no pause in continuity and no lessening of power.

Every ninety minutes, with infuriating regularity, the voice posed its unanswerable questions. There was no escaping it. In allegedly sound-proof rooms it came with the same clearness as in the open streets. Attempts to jam the broadcasts proved hopeless and, in a vain attempt to blot out the sound, the authorities resorted to the public address system. Garish music, military marches and the classics were poured forth at full volume. This too proved worthless; the frequency appeared to be tuned to the exact resonance of the normal ear drum and the voice could be heard clearly above the music.

"Is work easier for you to music or have you come to the reluctant conclusion that your technology is inferior to ours? Are your weapons and defensive equipment inferior? You do not know, your Supreme Committee does not know, yet, with your intelligence service provided only with a question mark, you are prepared to undertake an act of war. Do you, the individual citizen want war? It is your decision, not ours. Do you wish to co-operate with us to reclaim our heritage or do you wish the ultimate destruction which war will bring?"

As the voice had remarked earlier, all communities contained the good, the bad, the sane, the insane, the reasoning and the unreasoning. The good, the sane and the reasoning were already listening carefully and coming to conclusions.

They were aware that they were being subjected to one of the most skillful propaganda campaigns the world had ever seen, but they were equally alive to the fact that it was a campaign with its roots in truth.

The voice made no attempt to lead or mislead. It posed the questions and allowed whoever listened to supply the

112

answers himself. It was provocative but not aggressive, challenging but not destructive and the people began to think.

So obsessed was the Committee with stopping the voice, however, that they gave little thought to this angle until it was almost too late.

It was only when reports began to come in of street fights and some unfortunate person was killed in a brawl that they woke up to the danger in their midst.

Security was alerted and increased, informers encouraged, and a large number of likely individuals screened, paid high wages and returned to their jobs as plain-clothed vigilantes.

By this time, however, resistance was organised, secret cells were in operation and counter measures were already underway. Counter measures which carried on when the voice left off.

Slogans appeared on the sides of buildings, an incredible number of pamphlets were distributed and a large number of illegal transmitters went into operation.

Skeld, conscious that his position was precarious and anxious for reinstatement, became a member of the secret police.

To give him his due, he was thorough, single-minded and quite tireless. It was not long before he had a promising lead which he followed up with characteristic intensity. He knew he had a very big fish on the hook, but this time he did not make the mistake of trying to bring it ashore single-handed—he laid his findings and the evidence before the Supreme Committee.

Loom went through the papers slowly and carefully, then he looked up. "You are Skeld—yes—I remember you now. I think, and on behalf of the Committee, you have expunged your past mistakes. Mr. Skeld, this is a thorough and complete accumulation of positive evidence—see that this man is taken into custody immediately."

Skeld saluted and left, mentally rubbing his hands gleefully. His first catch and really big fish. Furthermore he was going to enjoy this—Pressly, head of Biology! More than once he, Skeld, had been the target for Pressly's quick temper and biting sarcasm. Pressly had once referred to him as a bumbling little bureaucrat whose intolerable interferences checked the course of true science.

He found Pressly, as he had expected, in his laboratory.

"You have some business here?" The biologist held a test tube up to the light, shook it, then replaced it in a rack.

Skeld smiled unpleasantly and leaned against the wall. The three men with him folded their arms and spread their legs, waiting his orders.

"Take your time, Director, but not too much time. You're wanted."

Pressly picked up another test tube. "I take it you have come to arrest me."

"It's customary with traitors—didn't you know?"

"A question of conscience, Mr. Skeld. A choice between insanity and humanity—which side of the fence are you?"

Some of Pressly's assistants laughed and Skeld flushed angrily. "I know you lot are all in this together, you're all under arrest. The charge is high treason. It is my duty to ask you come quietly but it is my fervent hope I am compelled to take you in by force—which way is it going to be?"

Pressly smiled. "Naturally we shall come quietly. Before we do so, however, I would like to draw your attention to the cage-like device in the roof of this laboratory. We call it an inhibitor. You will find similar devices in our living quarters, rest rooms and places of recreation. The purpose of these devices is to keep certain cultures restricted, that is to say, alive but not reproducing themselves by cellular division. Should the culture be removed from the influence of these devices, it will immediately start multiplying in a normal manner."

"What the hell are you driving at?" Skeld had the uncomfortable feeling that he was not only being mocked but that there was a catch somewhere.

Pressly smiled. "By an unfortunate mistake, I became infected by a certain streptococci some days ago and it is now in my bloodstream. Thanks to the inhibitor, however, the organism is unable to multiply, but should I be removed from its influence—"

He paused and did not finish the sentence. "Mr. Skeld, I am a carrier. I bear in my body the seeds of a highly toxic disease. Are you the heroic officer who is not only pre-

114

pared to lay his repulsive hands on my person but, at the same time, shoulder the responsibility for carrying an incurable infection into the streets?"

Skeld paled. "You're bluffing."

Pressly turned his back on him. "That could very well be true but dare you call that bluff?"

"I could blast you to pieces here and now."

"True—the characteristic moronic solution—but true. Can you be sure, however, that no fragment of flesh, no drop of infected fluid will not splash back in the explosion?"

Skeld found himself backing uneasily away, aware that his men were already slipping out of the door behind him. "I shall report this."

"By all means, this is out of your field, of course—good day, Mr. Skeld."

When he took the news to the Supreme Committee, however, he was shocked at the reaction.

"Pressly never bluffs," said someone in a worried voice.

Loom nodded tiredly. "It seems equally obvious that if Biology is heading the resistance, the Department of Medicine is in it with him." He sighed. "Gentlemen, we have no option but to concede, at least outwardly, to the pressure groups surrounding us. Perhaps in the subsequent negotiations, we may learn something of these Gadgeteers, their bases, numerical strength and so on. In the meantime, however, and if we are to survive, we must capitulate with outward good grace."

He looked down from his chair. "Mr. Skeld, my unofficial and unrecorded advice to you, is to get lost somewhere. You seem a loyal man so get lost with as many men of equal loyalty as you are able to find. When word is brought to you we shall expect you to act and, if your response is as forceful as we expect, you may rest assured of a seat in this Supreme Committee."

Back at Base 4, Ventnor had lived on his nerves for an entire week before signs of returning health became clearly determined in Judith's condition.

On the first day she had sat upright, he had tottered back to Gina and dropped heavily into the wide chair beside her.

115

"She's really getting better." Then, wearily: "My God, I feel like death."

She had pillowed his head in her arms. "I know, I know."

"You always believed in me, didn't you? You never doubted. I can't tell you what it meant."

"I *know* you." Then, anxiously, "You're exhausted, darling. You must rest."

He was not allowed to rest for long. Calls came in from every group in the world, not only in sincere appreciation but seeking advice and details for their own urgent problems.

So busy was he that he was only vaguely aware of the arrival of the Island ship and the events which culminated in open negotiations.

When the first vessel arrived at Base 5—others had gone to European, American and similar bases—he found time to go out with the others and see it arrive.

It meant very little to him until he saw the familiar uniforms and heard the harsh, if diffident, voices of the visitors. Then his mind went back to the pre-fabricated huts of the villages, the same people in the same uniforms dumping the piles of plastic clothing. He remembered the inspections, the punishments, the aloof God-like contempt, the death of his father and the bowl spinning like a top on the hard floor.

He forced prejudice from his mind with considerable difficulty.

Later, however, in conference with experts, he began to relax. The guards and inspectors who had come to the villages had clearly been of a special mentality and were not representative of the Islanders as a whole.

It was clear that the major problem was South American and his special talents were called upon.

The Island had already discovered that the presumed city of the sub-microscopics was surrounded by something. They presumed it was a force-screen but had been unable to discover any characteristic energy release. All they knew was that anything approaching it blew to pieces.

Ventnor was called upon to exercise his talents with his micro-robotics.

Prefabricated buildings began to rise round Base 4 and

experts from other bases began to come in from all over the world.

It was not long before the experts came to the reluctant and frightening conclusion that they were dealing with an intelligence far in advance of their own.

"Consider the problem of relativity," said one expert worriedly. "These things are masters of two time dimensions, by instruments or intelligence."

"Let us consider that in relation to our vulnerability," said another. "We must face the unpleasant truth that we are virtually defenseless against them. Furthermore, if they choose to attack us, their methods might be totally beyond us. They could invade us as individuals, pouring their units into our bodies like a conquering virus. They could dust the air with sub-microscopic mines which, when inhaled, could exploded in the lungs or in the bloodstream. Furthermore, taking the measurements of this alleged city and drawing a conservative picture in relation to their artifacts, they outnumber us by about twenty-eight billion to one."

Driven by urgency and helped by an uncountable number of experts, Ventnor produced another type of micro-robotic. These were conveyed in a thumb-size flyer to within a few feet of the presumed force screen and released in hundreds. Nearly all of them were destroyed, but those which survived brought back pictures.

The experts whistled and the majority of them forgot their scientific detachment. "My God, a mine field!"

The experts made no attempt to discover how they were anchored in the air. They could have been linked or suspended in some sort of magno-beam but if such was the case they were employing principles about which the experts knew nothing. The point was they were there, three layers of them, about a meter apart and so arranged they presented an impenetrable curtain.

Within limitations they had mobility. They moved to permit the passage of birds, rain drops and air borne dust to which, in comparison if they could see, must look like drifting mountains.

When approached by a powered vehicle, such as a spy probe, the net thickened at the point of approach until it was well-nigh impenetrable.

117

The mines themselves—presumably robotic instruments of limited initiative—resembled metallic potatoes into which innumerable small pins had been inserted. These 'pins' the experts assumed were the instrument's detection devices and detonation points.

The detonation of the mine itself was not only considerable but quite out of proportion to its size. A single explosion of such a mine was quite capable of blowing an eight centimeter hole in normal plate.

The vessel which had first found the aliens, although not armed but nonetheless insulated against air friction, had holes blown in it through which a man could crawl.

The mine was not restricted to self-destruction, however. Against Ventnor's micro-robotics they had simply released a bluish light which had effectively wiped them out of existence.

The experts shook their heads worriedly—many of them were beginning to look hunted.

At a large conference some days later, Loom, still clinging desperately to his reins of office said, heavily: "There seems only one answer. We must throw everything we have at it. We must blast a hole in this shield with every hydro-nuclear device to hand. We must follow with insecticides, incendiaries, cannisters of the most corrosive acids known to science and finally dust and re-dust the entire area with radio-actives. In short we must delete this area of South America from the face of the earth, if necessary to a depth of several kilometers so that nothing but an enormous crater remains."

Ventnor stood up flushed and angry. He was no longer the scientist, he was a specimen from the villages, remembering past wrongs and injustices and finding new ideals and new conceptions challenged.

"What the hell for?" He enquired loudly and belligerently.

Loom looked at him, recognized him and tried to erase him at a single stroke. "Who is this man—has he the authorization to be here?" Then more quietly. "The answer to such a question is surely too pointless for our attention, gentlemen, it is too obvious for discussion."

Ventnor stood his ground, still flushed and angry but now

in command of himself. "The only 'obvious' conclusion that I can arrive at, is that these intelligences have offered us neither violence nor offense. Any of my colleagues will support me when I say that these intelligences could have wiped us out years ago had they wished to do so. Not only have they all the advantages but they are about three thousand years ahead of us technically. On what grounds such dangerous policies? Provocation? Armed aggression? The right of another intelligence to live? I suggest it is fear, fear of the unknown, *superstitious fear* which surely has no place in a mind so devoutly in favor of the scientific detachment."

Far at the back someone cheered and clapped his hands. It was Matheson who was immediately taken aback when he found his uncontrollable enthusiasm supported.

There were cries of: "Here, here! Bravo! Well said!" and a wave of clapping.

"By God," said Prone, "the boy has fire. I never knew he had it in him."

Stein only smiled knowingly. "Our friend is old-fashioned. He believes in things."

"It's just as well he does. But for him our paranoic friend might have plunged us into something from which we could never have extricated ourselves."

Screens began to light, there was whole-hearted and absolute support from every base in the United States, from Europe, from Australia.

Loom clenched his huge hands, two bright spots of color in his cheeks. It was the first time in his life anyone had dared oppose him, let alone gain support. He was compelled to remind himself that these Gadgeteers favored a loose form of government once referred to as a democracy and not the efficient discipline of Island government. They were a menace, these people, they would pull the world down again to complete collapse.

He was by no means beaten. "I would remind those present that my opponent is hardly qualified to pass opinions on major issues of this kind. Not only is he completely out of his depth but he is also a deviant with a known glandular disbalance. It is not, therefore, surprising, that he should take up arms on behalf of a sub-microscopic life form since he, himself, can only be considered a true member of the human race by a considerable stretching of the imagination."

Stein jumped on him. "The President's genius for the complete distortion of truth is singularly illustrated here. Mr. Ventnor's plea was for sane conduct, not the military suicide which the President, in his obvious terror, so actively supports. As for the charge of deviance, this deviance was the stubborn determination of the human genes to remain normal in the race of spineless sheep which the President claims was being created for the foundation of new society. I, and my friends, have had some opportunity in the last few weeks of studying this alleged society. I put it to you, Mr. President, that somewhere along the road, the great ideal of Arnold Megellon was conveniently lost. You were creating not a stable society but a *slave society*. An army of zombies to reclaim the world while you lounged around on your island Olympus and gave the orders."

"That is a deliberate and malicious lie!" Loom stood up and shouted the accusation.

Stein only smiled. "Then the President will have no objection to an investigation, a committee of experts both from the Island and our own laboratories?"

Loom turned a dull red, his hands opened and closed but he was still a wily politician. "This is a deliberate red herring. You seek to distract attention from your very deliberate policies of negation."

He pointed his finger suddenly. "What does this alleged master of the sub-microscopic, this half-human specimen, intend? Are we, with his blessing, to hand over the world to an intellectual virus or does he, with a fanfare of heroics, intend to walk through this mine-screen and shake the first micro-organism he sees by the hand? No, gentlemen, he opposes, on extremely dubious grounds, that we fight to maintain a hold on our own planet."

Ventnor faced him calmly. "I propose, backed by experts from the Island and the Inland bases, building a number of sub-microscopic communication devices with which I hope to establish contact with these intelligences. Once we have done this we may draw conclusions on the policy of these life-forms and their intentions towards ourselves. We have,

120

despite the war-mongering of the President, suffered no overt hostility from these creatures. In point of fact, the very existence of a mine-screen suggests that this composite intelligence wishes only to be left in peace. Without being wildly optimistic who can say that genuine and sincere co-operation cannot be created between such widely divergent life-forms. At least it is a far saner solution than the suicidal assault which could very well result in the entire extinction of mankind."

There was an enormous cheer and an overwhelming burst of clapping.

The President rose, holding his cloak of office tight at the throat, then, staring stonily in front of him, strode out of the room. He knew he was beaten, discredited, but he maintained his appearance of dignity until he reached his own quarters. Once there, however, he knocked down one of his servants with a blow from his fist, retired to his private room and carefully tore his cloak to shreds.

When he regained his composure he sent a message to Skeld. It was an elaborate communication, full of pompous phrases and veiled suggestions but it boiled down to two words— "Get Ventnor."

The suggestion of communication, was enthusiastically taken up and Ventnor was almost overwhelmed by offers of help.

In a day or so several teams were working. Communication sub-microscopic robots were now no major problem and it seemed reasonable to suppose that light and sound were obvious mediums. Any intelligence, given time, could break down repeated light and sound signals into an understandable message. The real problem was a *relative* one —how fast? A code message fast in the macrocosm might, relatively, have intervals of several days between each 'blink' or 'beep'.

The experts decided on a message without break in the macrocosm but with detectable intervals in the microcosm. The message was taped, reduced, retaped, reduced again and fed to the micro-robotic carriers.

XIII

IN A MICROCOSMIC WORLD where airborne dust clouds drifted like asteroid belts, where every rain drop was a pear-shaped comet, they arrived and waited.

They circled in hundreds about two meters from the mine screen and blinked. Tiny shutters opened and closed over light sources; inconceivably small transmitters began to beam regularly— *"We are the instruments of macrocosmic intelligence."*

Submicroscopic diaphragms repeated the message in sound —"to establish contact between our two widely divergent life-forms—"

Blink—blink, blink—blink—*"to establish friendly relations, and, if possible, a high degree of co-operation beneficial to both our races—"*

In less than an hour later a dull green cube appeared suddenly among the communication robots and began to blink back:

"This vessel contains a recorded answer to your good-will message."

They picked it up, after considerable effort, in the thumb-sized vessel which had brought the micro-robotics.

As soon as they got it to the laboratory, however, it began to broadcast in standard morse with such power that it was perceptible—albeit as continuous sound—on high frequency receivers.

The experts recorded the sound, slowed it, re-recorded the slower version and slowed it again.

Finally they broke it down to dots and dashes.

THE INTELLIGENCES OF THE MICROCOSM (GELTHEA) WELCOME THE PEACE OVERTURES FROM THE MACROCOSM (MANKIND) AND APPLAUDS BOTH THEIR COMMON SENSE AND THEIR MATURE APPROACH TO AN ALARMING PROBLEM.

ALTHOUGH THIS PROBLEM WAS ONLY INFERRED, THE GELTHEA APPRECIATE THE DANGERS INVOLVED WHEN TWO ADVANCED INTELLIGENCES FIND THEMSELVES SHARING THE SAME PLANET WHICH BOTH REGARD AS THEIR OWN.

MANKIND, HOWEVER, NEED NOT CONCERN IT-SELF FOR LONG WITH THIS PROBLEM AS WITHIN A SHORT PERIOD (MACROCOSMIC TIME) THE GELTHEA WILL HAVE VACATED THIS PLANET.

WE ARE, RELATIVELY, AN OLDER RACE THAN YOUR OWN (THREE GENERATIONS PASS IN THE COURSE OF A MACROSECOND) AND EVOLUTION-ARY TRENDS HAVE WROUGHT MANY CHANGES.

ONE OF THESE CHANGES HAS BEEN A REDUC-TION IN SIZE WHICH HAS OPENED UP VAST NEW FRONTIERS FOR US.

TO ILLUSTRATE, YOU SEEK THE CONQUEST OF MACROSPACE. WE HAVE ALREADY CONQUERED MICROSPACE AND A VAST EXPANSION IS ALREADY IN PROGRESS.

TO US THE EARTH NO LONGER HAS SUBSTANCE. IT IS SIMPLY SPACE, AND ITS ATOMS SO MANY STARS, SO MANY SUNS, SO MANY GALAXES.

WE WERE ABLE TO CONTACT YOU ONLY THROUGH OUR REMAINING INSTRUMENTS BUT, IN VIEW OF THE MATURITY OF YOUR APPROACH, FELT THAT YOUR MESSAGE COULD NOT BE IG-NORED.

BY THE TIME YOU RECEIVE, AND ACT UPON, OUR ANSWER WE SHALL BE GONE AND OUR CITY DESERTED. MANY OF OUR RECORDS AND TECH-NICAL ACHIEVEMENTS HAVE BEEN PLACED IN A 'TIME-FIELD' FOR POSTERITY.

IT IS CLEAR THAT AVAILING YOURSELF OF THESE ASSETS IS WELL WITHIN YOUR TECHNICAL ABILITY AND WE WELCOME YOU TO AVAIL YOURSELVES OF ANYTHING WHICH MAY AID YOU.

THE GELTHEA.

The experts looked at one another, shaken.

"Thank God we used some sense over this."

"I'll say." One of them had a note pad covered with figures. "If we had thrown a missile at them it would have taken approximately—*their time*—nine hundred years to get there. They could not only have stopped it, they could have landed on it, got inside and perhaps altered the control circuit so that it came back at us. We've had a damn narrow escape."

"Been a bit of a false alarm all the same."

"Has it? We've been presented with a technology several thousand years in advance of our own and the Island and the resistance groups are working together."

"You have a point there—nothing like an outside threat to bring a big family together. What would we have done without our specimen? By the way, where is Ventnor?"

"He was here just now—no—wait a minute, didn't someone come with a message."

Someone had come with a message. It was brief, crude and to the point and Ventnor was already leaving the base.

Skeld, thinly disguised in a laboratory coat, watched him go and smiled thinly. Human nature didn't change, the strongest of men had a weak spot, emotions to be exploited. Tell a man you had his woman, tell him to come and get her alone. It was simple. The man knew, of course, he was walking into a trap but couldn't help himself.

"What the hell are you doing here?" said a voice.

Skeld stiffened, his hand jerking slightly towards his gun pocket. "Oh, it's you, Hobart. Thought you were still a prisoner." He smiled genially. "Glad to see you've got your freedom."

Hobart didn't smile back. "I was never a prisoner. They simply relieved me of my weapons and let me wander around. You haven't answered my question."

"Question? Oh, yes, security business, naturally."

"Whose security—mankind's or Loom's? There's no damn censorship here, you know."

"Don't tell me you've thrown in your lot with these Gadgeteers."

"Let us say I've seen enough to know when I've made a fool of myself. I've been through that recreator thing of theirs. I know what really happened."

"Mr. Skeld, I must remind you that you are still technically my subordinate. Kindly get out of my way, I have important business to attend to."

Hobart stood aside reluctantly then turned shaking his head almost knocking someone over. "Sorry! Good God, Matheson!"

"Well, well, it's been a long time." Matheson's mild gray eyes were neither friendly nor hostile.

"Listen, I haven't time to exchange pleasantries or recriminations. Something is going on." He repeated his recent conversation with Skeld.

"Is that all?"

"No, it's not all. Ventnor went striding out of the base about a minute before. He was as pale as death and looked worried out of his life. Skeld stood watching and was beginning to follow when I spoke to him."

Matheson's eyes narrowed. "It doesn't sound too good—What is it to you?"

Hobart flushed. "All right, I was smug idiot, I don't have to don sackcloth and ashes to prove it to myself or to you. Are we going to do something or not?"

"We are—catch."

Hobart caught the gun deftly. "Hadn't we better let the base know?"

"I intend to but I must tell them to be careful. This smells like some sort of trap. If the whole base goes after him, the opposition will blast him down out of hand."

Ventnor, now a mile from the base, strode over the rough ground almost unaware of his surroundings. *"If you wish to see your wife again come to Harthill Crossroads alone."*

He knew what 'alone' implied. He knew that Gina was not on the base and he knew that had he informed the base he would have been held there for his own protection.

There was no doubt that someone had her but he was fully alive to the fact that she was bait. He was walking into a trap.

Strangely he felt no regret. If they died, they would die together—could he ask more than that? Beside this, however, was an overwhelming fury that she should be hurt, that they should *dare*—

Half a kilometer behind, Skeld followed smiling to himself. It had been almost too easy. Occasionally he glanced back but he could see no sign of pursuit, not that he had really expected any.

Ventnor strode on. Above, the sky was a clear pale blue, a lark sang, the grass was bright with buttercups but he saw none of it.

He passed through the dust mounds which had once been Lenham, his mind filled only with one thought—haste. Not far now, Harthill Crossroads, where the assassin had been killed, where he, Ventnor, had been 'buried'. Why there?

He arrived forty minutes later.

A slim, dark haired man sat crossed legged on the ground. He had a weapon but the weapon wasn't pointing at Ventnor it was pointing at Gina.

"Stay right where you are, my friend. Don't move, don't try anything and this won't go off."

"Gina—Gina, darling, are you all right."

She stood unmoving but she smiled. "You shouldn't have come, dearest."

"I had to come, you knew it."

"It's a trap."

"I knew that too. I still had to come."

The man jerked the gun slightly. "Let us not become emotional, eh? Someone might move suddenly. This is an igniter gun or is the lady for burning?"

Skeld arrived some minutes later, slightly short of breath. "Ah, so you have them, Gelden. Excellent! I've waited several years to catch up with you, Mr. Ventnor."

"May I take him?" asked Gelden, hopefully.

"No, you may not—keep quite still. Mr. Ventnor—I like to go by the book, by routine. Since our specimen can no longer be 'marked' he must be disposed of in a routine manner." He pointed. "An old friend of yours, I believe."

Ventnor followed the direction of the pointing finger and stiffened.

He came striding steadily but unhurriedly across the grass—the dark suit, the round hat and the contrasting circle of white at the throat.

"Yes, you recognize him, no doubt. It's Padre 4, Mr. Ventnor. He, too, has been waiting a long time. He, too, has a duty to perform."

Ventnor felt a coldness inside him. He remembered the Padres in the villages, the people, the children, running for the huts as soon as they appeared.

He remembered the pursuit from Gret, the Padre, feet

126

apart, arms folded, staring down at him as he ran for his life.

It had been the Padre who had stirred the village against him, the Padre had wanted him dead.

Skeld sat down on a grassy mound. "He isn't armed," he said gently, "but then, Mr. Ventnor, neither are you. On the other hand, the Padre is very, very strong, too strong. Of course, you are a good deal faster but however fast you are the Padre will catch you. He's tireless. When you're tottering from fatigue he'll still be striding behind you and, in the end, he'll overtake you even if you have a fifty kilometer start."

Ventnor, although still frightened, was now coldly detached and in control of himself.

"Were you born a small time sadist or did you have to educate yourself up to it."

Skeld flushed but he said easily, "Save your breath, you're going to need it. Oh, and yes, play it heroic, your woman is watching. After all, you might save her, who knows—we shan't."

Ventnor took a quick step forward but the other waved his gun. "Don't lose the lady before you have to, sonny boy."

A minute later the Padre arrived and said: "Sir? you sent for me."

Skeld waved his hand. "Specimen/variant 225/9/446. You have your instructions."

The Padre turned his head slightly. "Specimen identified, sir; instructions, destroy."

The Padre turned, squat, brown-faced, expressionless, extended both hands and marched toward the specimen.

Ventnor, although cold with terror, instinctively dropped to the half-crouch of his intensive judo-training. Carefully he measured his distance, weighed the balance of his opponent, then he stepped adroitly to one side, grasped the wrist and pulled.

The Padre did a somersault and landed heavily on his back. There was, however, something frightening and unhuman in the way he climbed to his feet and came plodding back expressionless and implacable.

Ventnor, now fully conscious of what he was up against,

127

forced his mind to icy detachment. He must keep clear of those hands, if the Padre once got a grip he'd never break it.

He side-stepped again, kicking skillfully at the legs. The Padre went down again, this time on his face. Ventnor jumped high in the air and came down, heels first in the middle of the prone back.

It was a move that would have killed a normal man. It would have broken the back and ruptured the internal organs. The Padre made a faint grunting sound, rolled over as Ventnor sprang clear and climbed unhurriedly to his feet.

Skeld clapped his hands. "Quite a boy, aren't you, Specimen? Keep going, you'll get tired but the Padre won't."

The Padre came forward and Ventnor threw him again. This time he went high in the air and came down on his head.

The fall should have broken his neck but once more he climbed to his feet and came forward.

Ventnor was now panting for breath and his face was streaked with lines of sweat.

"Hot work, Specimen? Cheer up, its going to get hotter." Skeld was chuckling, softly.

Ventnor braced himself once more but before the other reached him, there was a curious thudding noise.

The Padre staggered, raised his arms slowly in a grotesque suggestion of benediction and fell forward on his face.

"What the hell!" Gelden was suddenly on his feet, gun drawn, peering nervously about him.

Ventnor, panting from exhaustion, stared down uncomprehendingly at his opponent. In the middle of the black cloth was a jagged and blackened hole into which he could have inserted his clenched fist. There was, however, no blood, no charred flesh. Synthetic flesh had burned away like cloth and beneath this was a cage, a rib case of bright shining metal, a mess of fused circuits and fine wire—the Padre was a robot!

"You were followed." Gelden was crouched but poised like an animal. "You incompetent fool!" He raised his voice. "Listen you, out there, if you fire one shot or try and take

128

us, we shall—" His shouting ended in a peculiar sigh and he rolled sideways and lay still.

Skeld flung himself sideways, his face ashen. The gun which had appeared suddenly in his hand, was menacingly steady.

"Don't move, you two, or I'll blast you down where you stand." He shouted, finishing Gelden's threat. "If you come in, I shall kill these two."

"No you won't, Skeld." The voice was Hobart's. "If you kill your hostages you've no insurance. Not only that but I shall take immense pleasure in killing you personally. I propose shooting you slowly to pieces, starting at your feet."

"Now look, Hobart, I have no quarrel with you."

"You have a quarrel with everyone but yourself, Skeld. I'm coming in."

"Don't do that." The voice was a little shrill. "I shall blast you down."

"If you're lucky. I'm somewhere in this long grass—where? Furthermore I have Matheson with me—somewhere —and to cheer you up, the base knows by now."

"Look, Hobart, give me a break, give me five minutes to get clear." Beads of sweat stood out on Skeld's forehead.

"Better get moving now, I'm on my way."

"Blast you!" Skeld fired wildly at the long grass. Yellow flame gushed upwards; clods of earth rose in the air; there was a brief swirl of smoke and then he turned and ran.

He ran until he was breathless, then he flung himself into a convenient hollow. As he did so, a hawthorn bush to his right suddenly vanished in a brief burst of vapor.

He looked back twice. Keeping his head down, he fumbled a caller from his pocket. "This is Skeld. I'm in a spot; get a fix on me, for God's sake. If you're quick you can get Ventnor too. There's only two men and a woman with him." He paused to fire again over the rim of the hollow. "Don't play—burn out the whole area and make sure."

A crisp voice said: "Message received, positioned fixed; we're on our way."

Skeld raised the gun, fired four times, then made a crouching sprint for the next cover. He made it but a smoking crater appeared suddenly at his side as he flung himself behind a grassy mound.

He lay still trembling and panting. Why didn't the ship hurry!

The ship did hurry. It came shrieking over the hills to his right, skin glowing redly from friction.

"Slow her, we're there."

"I know." The pilot was already braking.

"Fix," said the detector man crisply. "Right below us—pick him up?"

"Yes—no, no. There's a man and woman over there, must be the specimen."

"There's a couple of men stalking Skeld as well."

"We'll get the lot in one fell swoop, brother."

The detector man squinted downwards. "Shall we rub out that little group of primitives while we're at it?"

"What little group of primitives?"

"In among that clump of trees there—can't you see them? About six I should say, they seem to be carrying cross-bows."

"Ah, yes, I can just—*cross-bows!* Did you say cross-bows? UP! Get her up, gun it, kick it, *get her up!*"

"But Skeld—"

"To hell with Skeld. Those are not primitives, you blasted fool, they're the Maidstone boys from Base 4—where the hell have you been these last two months? Gun her up, damn you."

The ship lifted its nose wrenchingly, began to arrow upwards. Inside someone switched on a magnifier screen. "Got them—Good God, they're actually firing those things at us."

"No!" The voice was despairing. "Keep gunning it, Heald."

"You want this motor to blow? Every needle I've got is the wrong side of the red line already. This is a kite, not a missile."

"All right, *all right!* Horn, pick those arrows up on the screen, keep track of every damn one."

"Oh, for goodness sake, we're already hitting all of Twelve hundred."

"Yes and piling on acceleration at a kilometer second, I know that—*find those arrows or I'll blast you down where you stand!*"

"Okay, okay." Switches clicked. "Check—check—check—four arrows—check—falling behind at meter a second. In short, we're out-running them." He paled suddenly. "Say, those things are hitting all of fifteen hundred!" He made hasty calculations and when he spoke again, his voice was curiously hoarse. "They're twenty-one kilometers from point of release, and only ten kilometers behind us—what the hell are they?"

"Do I have to draw a diagram? They're pursuit missiles. Do you think I'm pushing this ship over the edge for amusement?"

"But they were fired from cross-bows!"

"What the devil does it matter how they were fired? They once pushed aircraft off the decks of ships with steam catapults. It was not only a highly effective method, but it gave the aircraft a boost—*keep track of those arrows.*"

"Right—" Pin pricks of moisture sppeared suddenly on his forehead. "They're picking up again."

"Which means once we're clear of the atmosphere completely they're going to pick up even more."

"What do we do?"

"We do the tightest turn this kite will stand, and plunge back into the atmosphere."

"Think we'll shake 'em?"

"Of course we won't shake them. Unless I'm very much mistaken they'll anticipate the turn and gain a couple of kilometers."

"Then what's the point?" The voice was shrill.

"You want to blow up in this thing? Can't you get it into your head that in the long run they're going to catch us. Our only hope is to get far enough into the atmosphere to use the emergency ejection sytem and bail out."

"At this speed!"

"Take your pick—strap in—turning five seconds as from now—one—two—"

Kilometers below, Skeld was still blasting in front of him and making short sprints for the next cover.

He had seen the ship arrive and inexplicably arrow skywards with a whine of emergency boosters, but he was too hard-pressed to think about it. He was aware of hatred, bitterness, a sense of despair but there had been no real time to think. He was conscious only of his own predicament. It was clear that Matheson and Hobart, using all the available cover were not pursuing him directly but on either side. He had, therefore, to keep retreating to avoid being outflanked.

As he flung himself flat in another hollow he became aware of something above him and had a blurred impression of something at a tremendous height which looked like a white-hot needle.

The ship! His rescue ship, coming down so fast that despite friction insulation she would probably burn up before she hit the ground.

The ship never hit the ground. At ten thousand meters the tail vanished inexplicably and then, suddenly, there was nothing but a huge cloud of swirling black and white smoke. Fragments fell out of the smoke, burning debris and then the smoke drifted away and there was nothing.

Skeld was compelled to make another sprint before he could take it in but by now his nerve was beginning to crack and he fumbled desperately in his pockets. Make a white flag of something, if he could draw those two swine out into the open—no, better surrender properly. He happened to glance upwards and experienced a wave of relief which made him feel slightly faint.

Several glittering things were drifting downwards. Safety pods! The crew had ejected before the ship blew. He counted eight but only four made the ground. Matheson and Hobart knocked the others out of the air despite vicious fire from side arms.

"Over here!" Skeld took care not to raise his head.

Three made it, the fourth man staggered in mid-stride then pitched sideways, smoking.

Somewhere someone arrived with an audio caller and a quiet voice said: "The battle is over. You are outnumbered by ten to one. Raise your arms above your head and stand up. There will be no reprisals and you will not be shot."

"They must think we're fools." Skeld's cheeks were quivering loosely.

"I don't know." Holt sounded uneasy. "They could be speaking the truth. There are Islanders among them."

"Think they'd care either? We're outlaws now, my friend.

"What can we *do?*"

"Look, if we can get up that hill a bit, we'll have the advantage of height. We could hold them off until darkness anyway." Skeld was almost pleading. "Once we're clear I can use the caller. Loom will see we're all right. He'll send a ship or something."

"Oh, very well." Holt still sounded undecided.

"You two break back, I'll lay down covering fire. When you're clear, whistle and cover me—you know the drill."

Skeld began to fire wildly and the two men raced back for a chosen place of concealment.

The voice said: "Be sensible. Give in, you are surrounded. Above all do not seek refuge up the hill. We warn you that there are concealed micro-weapons there. If you go up the hill we cannot save you."

Skeld laughed harshly. "They must think we're simple minded. They came down themselves when they first picked Ventnor up,·I know that for a fact." He looked back quickly.

"If we all made a break together, we'd probably make those small trees—come on."

Skeld and Holt made it but the third man fell on his face half way and did not get up.

Skeld beckoned. "Come on—they can't see us now and they'll be pretty wary of coming in to flush us out; we can keep going."

After climbing less than fifty meters, however, Skeld turned and frowned. "What's the idea?"

"I don't know what you're talking about." Holt had been glancing back over his shoulder in case of pursuit.

"You threw something at my back. I thought you were trying to attract my attention."

"Damned if I did."

"But I felt it—I can still feel it."

"Don't be—" Holt stopped, his face colorless, then, quickly: "I'm beaten, you go on while I get my breath, Mr. Skeld, catch you up in a minute."

"What the hell's the matter with you?"

"Nothing—nothing at all, Mr. Skeld." Holt took quick steps backwards.

"You're lying!" Skeld's gun was suddenly pointing. "Now you keep quite still and tell me what its all about, eh?"

Sweat stood out on Holt's face, his jaw quivered. "You—you're—you're a carrier." He swallowed and suddenly shouted. "There's a chase mine stuck right in the middle of your back!" He turned and ran. . . .

Back at Base 4, Prone said: "So Loom committed suicide?"

Stein smiled faintly. "Rumor has it that he shot himself in the back of the head which not only suggests extreme ingenuity but the final collapse of the old order."

Prone nodded and smiled. "Hello, here come the love birds. I expect you're glad they're safe." He watched Ventnor and Gina come into camp holding each other very closely. "I'm told you played cupid."

"Did I?" Stein smiled with one side of his mouth. "You forget I am also a psych. They are the first, others will follow, mankind is growing up."

"Candidly, I haven't a clue what you're talking about."

"Haven't you? Since man first stood on two legs, marriage has been hit and miss—usually miss. As I say, these are the first, others will follow."

"I'm still not with you."

Stein sighed. "There, between those two, is utter and absolute perfection, the identity of the one completely uniting with the other. There, according to my graphs, is the perfect union."

Prone shrugged. "Is it important?"

Stein smiled, gently. "You're a big man, my friend with big ideas. You're dreaming of reclaiming the world, of mighty engineering projects, of damming rivers and seeding deserts but even Arnold Megellon saw the need for something else."

"Well?" Prone still sounded puzzled.

"All your work would be in vain if the world fell to pieces again. On those two, my friend, and those who will follow them, you may rebuild your world, for only on such unions can mankind form a truly stable society."

Stein turned slowly and walked away.

134